Christmas Carroll

Crissy never thought to see him again; believing he wouldn't return to his home in Snow, Pennsylvania once he had left. Her hand shook as she lifted the coffeepot and slowly walked toward the dark-haired man sitting alone at a table meant for two. His back was bent; his hands at the sides of his face, as though holding his head up was the only thing he could manage.

He stared out the window of the Holly Café, totally ignoring her as she refilled his coffee cup.

"I'm sorry about your dad," she said softly.

One hand dropped to the table as he slowly turned to face her. A smile tilted his lips just slightly, but didn't reach his eyes—eyes the same mesmerizing blue, yet somewhat sadder than she remembered. He was as handsome as ever, but had the mature look of a man of the world. She tried to shut out the memory of the last time she'd seen him when she had cried, begging him not to leave; even though she had known for Nathan Roberts, there had been no other options.

He opened his mouth, then closed it without speaking, but he kept staring at her and Crissy wondered if he didn't recognize her. Then, he reached a hand to her hair, coming away with several strands of silver garland.

"Hello, Christmas Carroll," he said her full name in that deep, smoky voice she still heard in her dreams. "I see some things never change."

She laughed. "We're getting ready to decorate and I..." She stopped, wondering if discussing Christmas decorations was appropriate with someone whose father was fighting for his life. "Have you been to the hospital?"

"No, I just got into town, and I..." He swallowed, turning back to the window.

"Nathan." She sat down, placing her hand on his. When he had left town after high school, it had been on bad terms with his dad. Now, Crissy only hoped he had time to mend the rift. Before she could ask, he turned her hand in his, laying the silvery garland on her palm and curling her fingers around it. She felt his warmth, the light calluses on his fingers, and the old familiar wave of heat that used to sweep through her at a single glance.

"I have to go." He paused, tossing some bills onto the table. "Maybe I'll see you later." And he walked out the door.

They were both older and although she hadn't seen him in far too many years, Crissy felt like they had never been apart. Nathan was

4

Before Tomorrow Comes

A Collection of Favorites for all Seasons

By Barbara Baldwin

Amazon Print 978-0-2286-0619-2

BWL Publishing Inc.

Books we love to write ...
Authors around the world.

http://bwlpublishing.ca

her soul mate, and maybe before he left town this time, she could make him see that.

* * *

Hours later, Nathan pulled the collar of his coat up around his ears to block the cold wind as he stood in the dark in front of Poinsettia Place, trying to decide whether to knock. The house, red with white trim, was exactly as he remembered, as was the entire town. Old-fashioned lamps lit street corners; holiday decorations hung from every conceivable nook and cranny, and snow sculptures scattered the landscape from City Park to the outskirts of town. The whole damn town got into celebrating Christmas. That is, when the men weren't working twelve hour shifts in the mine. He swallowed hard. Or when there wasn't a mine accident like the one that left his dad in a coma.

He had refused to follow in his dad's footsteps and work in the mines after high school. Instead of being proud of Nathan for wanting to make something of himself, his father had never understood. He could still hear his dad's words from that long ago day.

"What's wrong with working the mines? There's pride in being a third generation Roberts miner. You too good for that?"

All he'd ever wanted was to shake the coal dust from his soul; to make enough money to buy his mom all the things she had done without. Only Crissy had understood, even as she had cried when he had boarded the bus for college.

The front door opened and Crissy stepped out, carrying a wreath. When she spotted him, her face broke into a bright smile.

"Hey," she said, "come on in."

He took the wreath and hung it on the door at her direction, then followed her into the house. Warmth surrounded him, a spicy scent heavy in the air.

"I see you're at it." In the living room, a large tree stood, lights already twinkling from the branches.

"Everyone has to be ready for the grand lighting ceremony on the twelfth. That's only three days from now."

The Christmas holiday dominated Snow. Businesses had names like the Holly Café, Noel Cleaners, and Candy Cane Pharmacy. Kids got a free day off school at the first heavy snowfall to create snow sculptures that dotted yards and roadsides. But the holiday was particularly special to the woman standing in front of him, hanging ornaments on the tree. Christmas Carroll had been born on Christmas day.

"This looks familiar." He lifted a round paper ornament from the tree, the youthful coloring nudging a memory.

Crissy blushed. "In fourth grade, I decided to dress up as a Christmas tree for our

Halloween party. You know, given my name and all."

He nodded. "Now I remember. All the kids laughed at you."

"Everyone except you. You made me this ornament and pinned it on my tree costume."

He stepped closer. "You were the prettiest Christmas tree I had ever seen in October."

"And you were my hero from that day on." She raised her head and his lips brushed her forehead.

Her sweet scent brought back other memories—their first kiss; high school prom; the night she gave herself to him with the promise to love him always. She had been his one regret in leaving all those years ago.

He wrapped his arms around her and lowered his head. Time had no doubt blurred his memories, because he didn't recall her body feeling this lush against his, nor the fire in his blood so hot from a single kiss. His tongue darted along the seam of her lips and she opened to him, her hands sliding around his waist to caress his back.

"Nathan." She whispered his name like a wish granted. He rained kisses down her neck, sucking lightly at the rapidly beating pulse in her throat. She pulled him closer. God, he wanted her naked beneath him. He raised his head to gaze into eyes the color of holly in the sunshine.

"What have you been doing all these years?" She caressed the side of his face as she spoke.

"Crissy, I don't want to talk." It was a bold statement and he searched her features for his answer. He needed her tonight.

* * *

Crissy's heart hammered at Nathan's words. His smoldering look told her how much he wanted her. Every year he had been her Christmas wish, but he never came home. So every New Year's resolution was to quit loving him but she had broken it within days of making it.

She took his hand and led him upstairs. The residents of Poinsettia Place were already in bed, and even though both were hard of hearing, she put a finger to her lips in caution.

"I wondered if you had the same room," Nathan whispered as she shut her door and turned the lock.

"Same room, same house, same girl," she replied.

Nathan's hands slid around her from behind, cupping her breasts and pulling her back against him. He kissed her neck, murmuring, "Definitely not the same girl."

Crissy's breath caught at his tender touch. She pushed against him and the fire that had started with one kiss burst into flames. She spun in his arms, lifting her mouth to his in a devouring kiss. Her hands shook as she unbuttoned his shirt, jerking it from his shoulders. She desperately wanted to feel bare skin.

Nathan tugged her sweater up and she groaned. "Hurry," she gasped, reaching for his pants. In seconds, they were naked, but as Crissy stared at the man from her dreams, she suddenly found she couldn't move. He was so gorgeous. He had always been tall, but now his chest had filled out; the muscles tight and lean. She reached out to touch him, smiling when he hissed as her fingers followed the sprinkling of dark hair down his chest.

"God, that feels so good," he groaned as he tucked his head against her shoulder.

Nathan had never intended to jump into bed with Crissy the moment he saw her, but memories had flooded through him. Where once a lithe, blossoming girl had shyly stood before him, now a lush woman was looking at him with such longing, his knees went weak. She leaned in and licked his nipple and fire shot through him. She tilted her head back and gave him a sexy smile.

"I know we have all night, but would it hurt to hurry a little this first time?"

This first time. Nathan scooped her up and turned to locate the bed. If he had his way, there would be a lot more than just this time.

He followed her down on the bed, his hips nudging her thighs open. He had thought that coming back to Snow wouldn't mean much, but

9

this felt like coming home. He greedily sucked one pert nipple. Her back arched, urging him on.

She lay seductively on the bed, her eyes devouring him, her tongue peeking out to lick her lips. It dawned on him that, first time or not, he wanted to savor the moment and give her the pleasure she deserved.

He lifted one of her knees, bending to kiss the sensitive skin at the inside, then licking it with his hot tongue.

"Oh, God," she groaned as he worked his way up the inside of her thigh. She reached down to tug on his shoulders. "Now!"

He had to chuckle. "Patience, Christmas. Good things can come more than once a year." Even saying that, he gave her what she wanted, sliding all the way inside her, groaning at her tightness. She wrapped her legs around his waist and he sank deeper. As his lips found hers and he began to move, he wondered how he could ever have left her—this—even in his quest to make something of himself. And then he couldn't think at all as pleasure washed over him when she clutched around him in orgasm, crying out his name. His hips jerked as he came so hard, it bordered on pain—an exquisite pain he would gladly take over and over again.

* * *

Crissy woke in the morning alone. She rolled over and stared at the ceiling, wondering if she had dreamed that Nathan had been there with her. He was like a ghost from Christmas past. Had she wanted him so desperately she had conjured him up? But no. The tenderness she felt was no dream. Nathan had shown her a piece of heaven.

The phone interrupted her thoughts. One of the waitresses had called in sick and they were busy. Most of the time, she thought as she dressed, she didn't mind her inheritance—the Holly Café and Poinsettia Place. The home where she had grown up had first been a Bed and Breakfast, then somehow drifted to having permanent boarders. Both places helped pay the bills and she really loved where she lived. But there were days...

"Young man, what are you doing? Why are you here? Does Crissy know you're snooping around her living room?" Crissy could hear Matilda Grumbley as she came down the stairs.

"Ma'am, I'm just trying..."

"Don't you ma'am me. I never married. Men aren't worth the aggravation. Don't look at me with that smug expression, Henry Holliday, you're just an old pain in the tush. Where is Crissy? She knows I have a doctor's appointment today."

Oh, Lordy, Crissy had completely forgotten. She hurried around the corner.

"Matilda, good morning," she said perkily, hoping for once this particular boarder would be in a good mood. She should have known better.

"You know I like to be there early. What have you been doing and who is this man?"

Crissy stole a glance at Nathan, whose eyes twinkled and whose smile defied her to tell cranky Miss Grumbley just exactly why she was running behind schedule. She could feel a blush heat her face.

"Matilda, give the girl a chance to speak, for heaven's sake." Henry spoke up.

Crissy smiled her thanks. "Henry, would you mind having your breakfast at the café? Jill's sick and I'm going over."

Matilda interrupted. "You know I can't be late."

Crissy ran her fingers through her hair, frustrated the day was starting like this. She turned toward the kitchen.

Nathan followed. "How do you do it? I can't find a WIFI connection and my cell doesn't even get a signal here."

"I'm sorry I don't have WIFI, but we usually have cell phone service. I'll call someone today."

"Honey, that's not why I said anything," Nathan cajoled. "Why do you stay here, with this?" Nathan gestured back to the living room where Matilda and Henry were still verbally sparing. "Don't you want more?"

Crissy stopped in the process of pouring a cup of coffee. Her parents had left her the café and their home—what more did she need? She tilted her head toward Nathan, who despite his good looks, appeared somewhat harried.

"What have you been doing all these years?" she asked the question he hadn't answered last night.

"Building a business and making money," he answered, sounding defensive.

"I'm not judging you, Nathan, but are you happy?"

"I can buy whatever I want. I have a condo in New York and drive a new car every year."

"But are you happy?" she asked again. When he didn't answer, she said, "Perhaps you need to be reminded what Christmas is all about."

His eyebrows raised and lowered and a sexy smile lifted the corners of his mouth. "Oh, I would say I found that out last night. And I wouldn't mind enjoying Christmas more fully again tonight."

"Sh, they'll hear you." She blushed. "Besides, that's not what I meant." She loved her name, but it did get confusing at times.

Crissy knew Nathan would have done anything to flee the coal mines, and basically, his heritage. Even though small towns weren't for everyone, she wondered if Nathan liked New York any better. She smiled as a plan began to form. A little reenactment of *The Christmas Carol,* with some minor character changes, might just be in order. "Would you do me a huge favor?"

His eyes narrowed. "I'm not sure I like the sound of that."

"If you'll take Matilda to her doctor's appointment, since you'll want to go see your dad, anyway," she hurried to explain when he started to protest, "I can cover at the café and everyone will be happy."

"Do I get a favor in return?" he murmured, stepping close to kiss her ear before trailing his hot wet tongue around the shell.

Crissy was willing to agree to anything if he kept tantalizing her senses. "I'll feed you," she suggested.

"Anything I want?" Hot breath fanned her hair, yet she shivered.

"Crissy, it's time to go," Matilda hollered from the living room.

She tried to pull away but Nathan held her tight.

"Crissy." Matilda's voice was getting closer.

"Okay," she said, prying his arms away, "anything you want."

* * *

Twenty minutes later, Nathan wondered if he had struck a bargain with the devil. He knew for sure Matilda Grumbley was the devil's mother. She complained about all her aches and pains, and practically everyone in town. Nathan had grown up here, and he knew the town wasn't that bad.

"Mrs. Grumbley, we're here," he finally interrupted.

"Don't be calling me Missus. I'm a Miss; always have been and always will be." She jutted her pointed chin in the air.

And I can see why. Nathan kept that thought to himself as he hurried around and opened the door, helping Matilda out and up the snowy walk.

"Be back in precisely one hour, young man. I don't want to stand around in the cold waiting for you."

"Wait inside if I'm not here," Nathan said.

"One hour." She walked past him into the reception room and Nathan turned to walk the short distance to the hospital entrance.

He wondered what had made Matilda Grumbley an old sourpuss. Apparently, she didn't have anyone to take care of her. As he walked down the sterile hospital corridors, he thought about his own life. He had family, although he wasn't close to them anymore. When he got old, would he have to rely on the goodwill of others? God, he hoped not. He couldn't imagine being as lonely and bitter as that old woman.

Nathan didn't get back to Crissy's until well after dark. Other than returning Matilda home precisely one hour after dropping her off, he had stayed with his mom at the hospital. The doctor had said Dad was slowly improving although he was still in a coma.

Later he had gone to the library to catch up on some work via the internet. He talked to his secretary—on a pay phone, for God's sake—and told his partner to take over when meetings couldn't be rescheduled.

Now, as he opened the door, Christmas music washed over him and the tension left his shoulders. He stomped his feet, numb from the cold, and shrugged out of his coat.

"Crissy?"

"In the kitchen."

He found her with an apron tied around her waist, elbow deep in flour. He thought how right she looked and wondered why she wasn't married with a houseful of kids. Even as he thought it, his chest tightened in jealousy over an imaginary husband doing to her what he had done last night.

That's stupid, he lectured himself. You have no claims on her.

"How's your dad doing?" She bent over to put a sheet of cookies into the oven and his mouth went dry at the sight of her tight, jean-clad bottom. As soon as he was sure she wouldn't burn herself, he grabbed her from behind.

She squawked, pushing against him to get loose. "Stop that. Henry and Matilda are in the other room." She continued to wiggle and it just made him harder. He nuzzled her neck, enjoying the homey smell of her.

"I checked; they're both asleep in front of the TV. Besides, I think Matilda could use a little voyeurism. It might improve her mood." He finally released her when she reached into the warming oven for a plate piled high with roast and potatoes.

"What's with her, anyway?"

Crissy put the plate on the breakfast bar and he sat, digging in as she began cutting out more cookies. "She's just old and lonely."

"Yeah, well, she's going to stay that way. Hell, all she did was complain about everything," he said around a mouthful of food.

"From what I heard, she moved here because of her fiancé. But he died in the mines and afterward, she devoted herself to teaching. She never married." She looked up from the dough she was sprinkling with colored sugar, her eyes searching, her expression serious.

"What?" He shook his head in confusion. "There's a message in there somewhere?"

"I just think there's more to life than work, that's all." The timer dinged and she turned to take the cookies out, replacing one sheet with another.

"You work hard. You run your dad's café, and you've turned your home into a boarding house for crotchety old people."

She gave him a soft smile. "I love what I do. I get to talk to people all day and Matilda and Henry need me."

"I need you," Nathan said, giving her a wolfish grin. "Besides, after having to cart Miss

Grumbley around, you owe me." He stood, slowly circling the breakfast bar. Crissy backed away.

"I promised you a meal. You got it." She pointed to his empty plate, but there was a twinkle in her eye and her luscious lips tilted into a sexy smile.

"That was delicious, but it wasn't what I had in mind." Nathan pressed against her. She was warm and soft and he ached with need. He nipped her neck, nibbling his way to her ear while his hands found the ties to her apron, dropping it to the floor so he could slide up under her shirt.

"The cookies," Crissy murmured, then groaned as he covered her breasts with his hands and her lips with his. She tasted and felt like heaven. He rubbed his thumbs across her nipples. When he ran his tongue across her lips, she opened for him and he tasted the essence of Christmas, but it still wasn't enough.

He reached for the button on her jeans, only to have the oven timer ding in his ear.

He groaned as he released her. "Get them out—fast—because I have something just as hot for you to handle." As soon as she put the cookie sheet down, he grabbed her hand and dragged her out of the kitchen.

"Those cookies ready to eat?" Henry called from the living room.

"The cook has disappeared," Nathan answered, "but help yourself."

Henry chuckled and Crissy swatted at Nathan, but didn't pull away as he urged her up the stairs.

* * *

Crissy loved Nathan's take-charge attitude. She had longed for someone to want her for herself and not for cooking a meal, meeting payroll or acting as a chauffeur. She was more than willing to give what Nathan demanded from her. And tonight, he didn't seem inclined to wait.

The minute her door was closed and locked, he had his hands on her shirt, pulling it over her head. She was naked before he had even kicked off his shoes, but when she protested, he backed her up to the bed and lowered her on it. He bent over her, arms braced on either side, and she felt her skin warm under his intent gaze.

"Now, I'll show you what I'm really hungry for," he whispered as he began kissing her, starting at her forehead, but never lingering long at any one place. She reached up to unbutton his shirt, but he placed her hands back on the mattress. "Tonight, I'm going to take care of you."

His kisses got hotter and longer as he worked his way down her body. Heat shot out from her breasts as he sucked one into his mouth, gently kneading the other. Her nipples tightened under his tender touch and she arched her back, wanting more.

His hands were everywhere, caressing, stroking, and heating her with a fire that centered deep within her. She could feel him through his pants, and she pushed her hips against him.

"I was just going for dessert." He nipped her nipple one last time before trailing his hot tongue down her belly.

Crissy groaned, knowing where he was heading and unable to protest. It just felt so good. The tingling anticipation made her ache. She wanted him to hurry and at the same time, go slow so she could savor every touch, every shot of electricity through her body.

Nathan stared down at Crissy. She was beautiful when she let herself go in the throes of passion, and he quickly pulled her to the very edge of the bed, groaning as he filled her completely. Then he stilled, savoring the clutch of her muscles around him. He started moving in long, slow strokes. Her eyes drifted open and he captured her gaze, wanting to imprint himself on her mind and heart; perhaps her very soul. His body was screaming for release but he held off until he felt her muscles squeeze around him again.

He watched as her eyes dilated with passion, her chest heaving with every gasping breath, and he knew this was the picture of Christmas he would carry with him forever.

When she called out his name this time, he came with her and it shook him to the very core.

Much later, with Crissy curled in sleep beside him, Nathan reflected on the course of his life, his family, Crissy and her happy outlook on life. Something had happened tonight. He wasn't sure if he had given it or if she had just outright stolen it, but his heart and soul were no longer his own.

* * *

Always an early riser, Nathan was already having coffee by the time Crissy came into the kitchen. She looked tousled, well-loved and very kissable as she yawned and stretched.

"Morning."

She spun around with a squeal. One hand flew to her chest and the other began a mad finger combing of her hair. Nathan shook his head as he walked toward her. He had watched her sleep this morning, her mouth open in a delightfully feminine snore and her short hair sticking out in all directions. But a smart man knew when to keep his mouth shut.

Instead, he bent to kiss her, wrapping his arms around her in a hug. "It snowed last night. I'll shovel the walks before I go to the hospital." He chuckled at her look of surprise as he grabbed his coat.

"Hello, who are you?" a young girl asked, standing on the back steps when he opened the door.

"Better question, how did you get here?"

She waved in a vacant manner. "Crissy had the idea to tie a rope from her porch to ours because I come over here so much." She grinned, showing braces.

"That's a pretty smart idea," Nathan answered, thinking how easy it would be for a youngster to get lost if it were snowing.

"Is Crissy here?"

"Hey, Megan, how come you're out so early on a Saturday?" Crissy peeked around Nathan, her hand lightly touching his shoulder and he thought how right it felt.

The girl held up a wad of yarn with needles sticking out of it. "I think I dropped a stitch but I can't tell." She then leaned forward and whispered, though loud enough for Nathan to hear, "Who is he?"

Crissy smiled. "Sorry. Megan Appleby, this is Nathan Roberts. Nathan, Megan is Polly's daughter. Polly was a classmate of ours."

The girl stood in front of him with her hand outstretched. "Is he handsome, Crissy?" Megan turned her head to the side where Crissy had been, but now had moved back inside. Before he could say anything, Crissy smiled and slightly shook her head.

"I think so," she said, answering Megan's question, "when he's not frowning." Then she grinned, sticking her tongue out at him. He took a step toward her but she put a hand on his chest.

"Megan and I have Christmas presents to make. If you insist on shoveling the walk, at least get Henry and go to the hardware store for some coveralls and goulashes." When he started to protest, she added, "You don't have to work in the mines to dress appropriately for the weather. Besides, Henry commented yesterday he needed nails for the birdhouses he's making."

As they walked away, Nathan listened to Megan chatter about the scarf she was knitting. *She's blind. Doesn't that make a difference?* He looked across the yard where a path zigzagged through the snow, a rope swaying in the breeze at about waist height.

Amazing. He had known Crissy was special, but he was beginning to see the impact she had on people she cared about. He smiled as he went in search of Henry.

* * *

Later as he and Henry sat in the café drinking coffee, he wiggled his toes in his new boots. He had to admit they were warm, but swore if his partner saw him, he'd laugh. He was a khakis and loafer kind of guy, even in winter.

"So what did you do before you started building birdhouses?" he asked Henry.

23

"I was in the stock market—made millions—but I'll tell you, young man, all the money in the world doesn't mean squat if you don't have someone in your life to share it." He got a faraway look on his face. "All that money couldn't help my Hettie one little bit when she got sick." He shook his head sadly, then took a sip of coffee. "Anyway, now I do a little woodwork to pass the time, but it sure does get lonely."

"Have you ever thought of marrying again?" Nathan asked.

"Ah, Hettie was my one love, but I wouldn't mind having a little fling now and again." He gave Nathan a purely male grin as he leaned closer. "You know, I'm thinking Matilda could use a good loving."

Nathan choked on his coffee. "Miss Grumbley?" he sputtered and the old man nodded. Hell, Henry had to be at least sixty-five, maybe seventy. How could he…Nathan didn't even want to go there. Yet when he thought about making love to Crissy for the next thirty years, he grinned.

Henry nodded. "Maybe I'll sneak into her room one of these nights and jump her bones. Whatcha think?"

Nathan grinned wider, lifting his hand in the air and Henry gave him a high five.

* * *

24

Crissy had just finished payroll when Nathan walked into her room. She closed her ledger and slid it to the back of the small desk.

"Are you hungry?" she asked, turning in her chair. "I can make you a sandwich."

"No, I ate with Mom." He walked toward her and Crissy couldn't gauge his mood. When she lifted her hand, he took it, playing with her fingers but obviously preoccupied.

He squatted down in front of her. "Dad's awake."

"Oh, Nathan, that's wonderful!" She was really happy for him.

"Yeah. We talked—really talked. All those years of misunderstanding were all about pride."

She brushed his hair back from his forehead. "Yours, or his?" she asked tenderly.

He gave her a quirky grin. "Both. I wanted to show him I could make it, and he wanted me to know that, working in the mines or not, he could provide for his family. I wrote, you know, and once I started working, I sent money. The money was always returned and it made me angry that he wouldn't take it, if only to make things easier. But it wasn't until today that I ever thought about the letters."

"Letters?" Crissy asked.

"Yeah," he said. "He sent the money back but never the letters. Mom says he still has them."

Crissy reached down and hugged him. "Oh, Nathan, he might be stubborn and proud, but he does love you. And you're just like him."

Nathan stood and tugged her to her feet. His kiss made her feel treasured and she wondered how she was ever going to stand it if he left her again.

Nathan slowly undressed her, planting kisses on each inch of exposed skin. Crissy didn't notice the coolness of her bedroom as Nathan warmed her body with caresses, and then with his own heat. Tonight there was no torrid sex as they'd had for the past two. Instead, they took their time exploring each other, savoring each kiss, even as the passion built. And when he gently took her to the heavens and beyond, Crissy's heart ached with love.

* * *

Monday was Crissy's day to work at the Holly Café, so Nathan spent the morning at the library checking email and doing business, visited his dad at the hospital, then came back to Poinsettia Place to prepare some reports. He was working at the kitchen table when the back door banged open and Megan stomped in.

"Whatcha doing, Nathan?" she asked, tossing her coat at an empty chair, then unerringly finding him at the table.

"How did you know it was me and not Miss Grumbley?" He was fascinated with her abilities, and with the fact she seemed to have such a happy disposition.

She wrinkled her nose. "It's your smell."

"I don't smell," he retorted, though he knew she meant scent.

She just laughed. "Will you take me downtown?"

He frowned at the graph on his computer screen, wanting to finish the report. "Wait for Crissy. She'll take you."

"I can't, silly. I have to buy her Christmas present. Mom's working at the store, so I can stay with her if you'll just take me. I have to get Crissy something special because she always helps me with my homework and she taught me how to knit. She's a really great person. And she's pretty, too, isn't she?"

Nathan laughed, realizing Megan was playing matchmaker. "Get your coat, squirt, and we'll go."

Megan kept up a steady stream of chatter as they bundled up and Nathan drove to the town square.

"Have you got your Christmas shopping done?"

"No."

"You'd better hurry. What will you get Crissy? You should get her something nice because she really likes you. I can hear it in her voice."

27

Nathan pulled into a parking space. He didn't need to be convinced that Crissy was someone special, but apparently Megan saw things he didn't.

She skipped beside him. "Isn't the snow beautiful?"

Before he thought, he said, "But you can't see it."

"Oh, but I do," she replied with feeling. "I didn't go blind until I was five, and besides, I see with my other senses." She grabbed his coat sleeve, pulling him to a stop.

"Close your eyes."

"Megan, we—"

"Just do it." She tugged his arm.

Nathan sighed, complying. "Okay."

"Now, what do you see?"

"Megan, I can't see."

"Then you're not trying."

Nathan decided if they were to get out of the wet snow and cold, he'd better come up with something. And just like that, he realized what she was talking about. Wet snowflakes landed in freezing spatters on his face as he tilted it upward. The cold was seeping through the soles of his shoes. As he opened his senses, he heard the scrunch of tires on snow, and the chatter of people walking by. He stuck out his tongue to catch the frozen drops of moisture and laughed right out loud.

"Megan Appleby, now who are you dragging around to see through your eyes?"

Nathan's eyes popped open to see a petite woman standing at the door of a small shop.

"Hi, Mom, this is Crissy's boyfriend, Nathan."

Even at thirty years of age, Nathan liked the sound of that. Still holding his hand, Megan dragged him into the store.

"Nathan Roberts, I never thought to see you back in Snow." Polly took his hands and squeezed. "How's your dad doing?"

Everybody knowing his business was one of the things he had hated in high school, but now the concern people showed felt refreshing.

"Megan," Polly turned toward her daughter, "there's a snack for you in the fridge behind the counter."

Nathan watched Megan bounce around the corner, never bumping or knocking anything off the shelves. When he turned back, he found Polly watching him. He felt his face heat.

"It's okay," she said, smiling. "I decided when Megan became blind due to a fever, I wouldn't treat her differently, nor allow it from others. But I couldn't have managed without Crissy."

"Nathan came to Snow to see Crissy," Megan called out.

Her mother smiled indulgently. "Crissy says Megan reminds her of Tiny Tim from *The Christmas Carol*. She always has such a positive attitude; as if there's nothing she can't do." Polly shook her head slightly. "I wanted her independent, but sometimes…"

"Oh, this scarf is so soft. Crissy would love it. Nathan, what color is it?" Megan came hurrying toward them.

"Megan," her mother warned.

Nathan just smiled. Turning to Megan, he took the scarf, sliding it across her outstretched hands. "It has swirls of color running through it—the blue of the sky and the green of leaves in spring. And there's lavender—a touch sprinkled here and there like fairy dust."

"See, you can do it," Megan whispered to him. Then she tugged him down and kissed his cheek. Nathan felt his heart burst open.

* * *

Crissy was totally shocked when she turned and saw Nathan herding Matilda and Henry into the Holly Café ten minutes before the lighting ceremony. Then he walked right up and gave her a kiss and love overrode everything else.

"I get the message," he murmured as he hugged her tight.

She frowned. "What message?"

Nathan waved toward Matilda and Henry, who sat at a table by the front window, for once not arguing. "Grumpy Christmas past and lonely Christmas present." He tilted her chin with a gentle finger, gazing at her with dark, passionate eyes. "I don't want to be like them."

Crissy's eyes filled with happy tears. "You always did catch on quickly, but what about Christmas future?"

"Tiny Tim is with her mother. As for our future, I want—"

"It's time!" One of the customers called when the courthouse clock began its deep, lingering gong.

Crissy grabbed her coat and Nathan's hand, hurrying outside, admonishing Matilda and Henry to stay inside out of the cold. They'd still be able to see the lights from the café windows.

Nathan stood behind her on the sidewalk, his arms wrapped around her, his breath a warm caress at her ear.

"I still don't see how you got Matilda downtown." Crissy shook her head.

"I called her Mrs. Scrooge."

Crissy twisted around to stare at him. "You didn't!"

He nodded. "I told her as long as I'm around, she would not be cranky or I'd sic the ghost of Christmas past on her." With that, he kissed her cheek. "There's only one gong left. You'd better look out that way." He nodded across the street.

As long as I'm around. Crissy said a swift prayer. She hoped that would be indefinitely.

As the last stroke of the courthouse clock echoed in the frosty winter night, the whole town of Snow became lit for the Christmas season. The giant tree on the courthouse lawn was a rainbow of color, and the huge star at the very top shone in the night as snow began to fall on the gathered crowd. Someone started singing, and soon the entire town burst forth with a boisterous rendition of Deck the Halls. As Nathan hugged her and his deep voice joined hers, Crissy wondered if this would be the Christmas she had always imagined.

* * *

Nathan couldn't wait to get Crissy alone, but for once Matilda was in a congenial mood and seemed inclined to visit. *That's what I get for being nice to her.* Nathan scowled across the living room, wondering if he should have spiked her eggnog.

"See what happens?" Crissy whispered in his ear. "You completely changed her outlook."

"Can I change her back?" Nathan pouted, wondering how long they would be held hostage.

"Patience. Isn't that what you told me?" Crissy asked, but when he glanced her way, he could see in her heated gaze that she was having just as much trouble focusing on the conversation.

"I was never patient. I used to peek under Mom's bed for presents. I always wanted my Christmas to come early." He narrowed his gaze meaningfully and was gratified to see her squirm.

"Are you alright, dear?" Henry asked. "You look a little flushed."

"It's been a long day. I think I'll call it a night." She began collecting their cups and dessert dishes.

"I'll get those," Nathan said as he stood. He watched as she started up the stairs, her hips swaying suggestively. He gritted his teeth, hoping he could join her quickly.

"Henry and I have been talking," Matilda said from directly behind him.

Nathan groaned, not bothering to hide his exasperation as he glanced over at Henry, who was smiling broadly. That dirty old man has been making it with Miss Grumbley.

"Young man." Matilda poked his arm to get his attention. "Since Christmas' parents have passed on, we've looked after her. And we've decided if you're going to keep hanging around here, then you must marry her. We don't believe in hanky-panky between young people." She gave a short jerk of her head and harrumphed.

Nathan opened his mouth to protest, then snapped it shut. Matilda had just given him his excuse. "You're absolutely right. If you'll excuse me, I'd better go ask Crissy right away."

He didn't wait for a response but bounded up the stairs two at a time. When he let himself into her room, his eyes quickly adjusted to the light from a single candle and he found her laying on the bed, gloriously naked, the candlelight shimmering off her pale skin.

"I wondered how long it would take you to make up an excuse," she said as she propped herself on one elbow to look at him with sexy interest.

Nathan undressed in record time, his eyes on Crissy and hers following his hands. She began squirming, her hips lifting suggestively as he walked toward the bed.

They came together, lips searching, hands stroking, and Nathan found her wet and ready for him. But she had other ideas.

"Lay back," she murmured, pushing against his chest. She straddled him then bent low for a kiss.

"Whatever you have in mind, you'd better hurry," he gasped.

"There's twelve days until Christmas," she teased as she peppered his chest with hot, wet kisses before sliding lower.

"Honey, that's twelve days of Christmas, and I plan on getting my fair share." His voice cracked at the end when she suddenly bit the tender skin of his hip.

"Of this?" she murmured.

"What do you want me to do, beg?" Nathan groaned as she continued to nuzzle him in all the most private places.

No, I want you to stay forever, Crissy thought but she wouldn't ask. He had to be willing to do it for his own reasons, and she could only hope that loving her was one of them.

When she couldn't stand the achiness any longer, she straddled him and lifted her hips.

"Wait," he gasped.

She shook her head. Capturing his gaze, she gave him her most dazzling smile as she slowly sank onto him. He filled her completely and as his hips began to buck, she longed for her love to be enough to keep him.

Nathan slid his hands from her waist up to her breasts and Crissy covered his hands with hers as he gently kneaded her flesh. Her head fell back, her hips undulating as he moved faster and faster.

"Nathan," she gasped his name, pushing one hand downward until he knew what she needed and moved his thumb to rub that singular pressure point that made her writhe with pleasure. She squeezed her thighs as he pushed deeper, triggering her climax. Pulsing sensations robbed her of breath, and each time her muscles clutched, Nathan thrust, sending her over the edge.

When she cried out, he plunged deep one last time, his hips arched, his face a mask of sensuous pleasure. She could feel him deep inside, and the thought of him filling her with his very essence caused her to climax again, squeezing around him to take everything he had to give.

* * *

When Nathan could breathe again and control his shaking muscles, he bent his legs, planting his feet on the bed to form a backrest for Crissy. He wasn't about to let her move anytime soon.

"Close your eyes and tell me what you see," he commanded when she finally looked at him.

"You've been talking to Megan."

"Just do it." He held onto a small ray of hope that she still loved him after all these years. Granted, they had just had the most phenomenal sex of his life, but he wanted more from Crissy. And he couldn't plan his future until he knew how she felt.

She gave him a smile, but complied, holding out her hands. He entwined their fingers as she began to speak. "I see a man who's too wonderful for words—and much more wonderful than he gives himself credit for. I feel sunshine warm my skin whenever he smiles at me, and I taste the flavor of our love in every kiss."

Then she opened her eyes, capturing his gaze as she slipped her fingers free to place his hand over her fast beating heart. "Most importantly, I can hear my pounding heart, telling me to love you well, and forever." She brought his other hand up and kissed his knuckles.

The tightness in Nathan's chest relaxed and he smiled. If he had known so many wonderful things would happen by coming home, he would have done it a long time ago.

"They say Dad will be home by Christmas," he said, thinking that would be a great time to get married.

Crissy frowned. "Will you be here at Christmas?" Nathan felt her heart start to pound beneath his hand and realized she needed reassurance, too.

He gave her a wide, teasing grin. "Honey, I love you and if you'll just get me internet access, I'll be here permanently."

She wiggled her hips, causing him to groan. "It was connected this morning."

Restoration of a Broken Heart

Molly walked through the rooms of Maple Manor, an Antebellum mansion, stopping in one room to soak up the feeling of history in the frieze along the ceiling, the floor to ceiling windows and the flocked wallpaper peeling from the corners. The workmen hadn't started restoring this room yet, but from what she had seen of the rest of the mansion, the renovations would be beautiful as well as historically accurate.

She loved American history and had always wanted to run a Bed and Breakfast, but she didn't know much about the restoration process. That's why, on the advice of her real estate broker, she had hired the reputable firm of Mallory Preservation Contractors, who were local but well known.

She knew her love of history and wishful thinking about owning a B&B wouldn't pay the rent. That was where her expertise came in. She knew people and marketing. The website was up and brochures had been shipped to travel agencies. Now, she was working on the costume ball for the grand opening of Maple Manor, just two months from today. That left a lot of work to do.

She had already opened for business on a small scale since most of the fifty-room mansion was already restored, including the dining room, several suites, and the music room, which had a mahogany bar discretely located off to one side in an alcove. The contractors were keeping the original décor as much as possible, and all the serving staff and concierge wore period clothes.

She wanted Maple Manor to be more than an upscale Bed & Breakfast. She hoped people would enjoy the relaxing and luxurious atmosphere of a by-gone era, and she looked forward to making her investment pay off by hosting small conventions and retreats along with having individual guests.

She had invested her entire divorce settlement, such as it was, into the place, hoping to make a new life for herself in the historic town of River Bluff. Contrary to its name, it actually nestled on the banks of the Mississippi River, not a bluff. Wide veranda doors at the back of the mansion opened to a beautiful garden where a sidewalk meandered through rose bushes and flowerbeds until it finally ended at the river's edge.

Molly walked into the music room, taking in the subtle lighting, the dark velvet curtains and the French Rococo furniture, original pieces that had come with the place. She noticed they even had a few guests visiting over drinks at several of the small tables.

"Good evening, James," she said to the bartender. "May I have a glass of wine, please?"

"Yes, ma'am, Ms. Bonner," he replied.

She turned at the sound of laughter, spying a group of men over in one corner. Taking in their work clothes and boots, they didn't look as though they belonged here, but she wasn't about to kick out paying customers.

Molly took her drink to the other end of the room, sitting in one of the balloon-backed side chairs placed by the window so guests could enjoy a view of the gardens. When her broker had sent her information on the mansion and she had toured it, she had fallen in love with the river and the friendly people in the small town. Although she had wanted to be as far away from LA and her ex-husband as possible, she had decided half way across the country was as good as being on the opposite coast.

"May I join you?" A man's voice interrupted her thoughts. He stood beside her chair, tall and tanned, the plaid shirt he wore rolled back to the elbows to show muscular forearms. He had salt and pepper hair and the bluest eyes she had ever seen. Eyes that were twinkling down at her.

"If I say yes, do you win the bet?" she asked.

He laughed. "You seem to have me pegged." He glanced back to the group of men in the corner. "What if I told you I wasn't with them?"

"Too late, I saw you talking."

"Oh." He looked disappointed, yet he continued to stand there.

Molly had come to the river to start over, perhaps even to have an adventure, and she supposed it wouldn't hurt if he sat down. Even as she told herself that, her heart beat a little faster and her stomach clinched. Of course, it didn't have to go any further than sharing a drink and a little conversation.

She put out her hand. "Hi, my name is Molly."

His large hand was warm and calloused when he clasped hers.

"Hi Molly, I'm Joe." He sat down and ordered them both another drink.

They end up closing down the bar, talking and sharing stories as though they had known each other all their lives. They both had an avid interest in history, though she preferred colonial and he liked the Civil War period. Where she was a transplant, as he called her, he had lived by the river his entire life, if not at River Bluff, than other towns along the waterway.

Given the type of music they liked and their discussion on today's youth, Molly figured they were about the same age. Of course, he politely refrained from asking and she wasn't about to tell him she had recently celebrated her forty-third birthday alone because her husband was with his new girlfriend.

"Are you staying here?" he asked when they got up to leave.

She hesitated. If she said yes, would it sound like an invitation? Was she ready to take her wish for adventure to the next level? She had been out of the dating scene for so long, she no longer knew how to interpret verbal nuances.

"I only want to walk you to your door, or see you to a cab," he said, "to make sure you're safe."

So much for her interpreting skills, she thought, trying not to feel disappointed. He was acting like a perfect gentleman, but somehow in her dream adventure that wasn't what she wanted at all.

"I have a room here," she answered, "so it's perfectly safe."

"You never know," he replied, a twinkle in his eye as he took her elbow and ushered her out the door. "There are all kinds of unsavory characters working on the renovations here, just waiting for the chance to take advantage of a lovely woman who's all alone."

"Does it show so very much?" she asked him.

"Only to someone just as lonely."

He took her passkey and slid it into the lock at her door.

"Night, Molly." He handed her the key. When she didn't immediately move, he touched a finger to her cheek, sliding it gently down to the corner of her lips.

"Sweet dreams."

And he turned and walked away.

* * *

It was four in the morning and Molly had yet to fall asleep. She plumped the already plump pillows and turned over just as the room phone rang.

"Do you want to get some breakfast?"

She recognized his voice. It was the same deep baritone that had been running through her head since he had walked away from her door.

She laughed. "It's four in the morning."

"Oh, were you sleeping?"

"No."

There was a pause on the end of the line.

"Molly, I want to see you."

Her heart skipped a beat and she couldn't think of anything to say. It had seemed forever since a man had paid attention to her, and she was almost afraid to trust her instincts about Joe.

"Why?"

"Because I'm hungry."

She laughed again, a carefree feeling running through her body that she hadn't had in a very long time.

"No, I didn't mean breakfast. I meant why do you want to see me?"

"Because I'm hungry," he said again.

She sucked in her breath, a delicious sensation spreading through her. She thought about her life. She was a middle-aged career woman who had always thought well of herself until her husband found he liked young secretaries better. It wasn't a new story, but this time it was her life, damn it, and it hurt. Now, here was Joe, a handsome man who found her interesting. Was it fair to use him to regain her self-esteem?

"I don't think I'm ready for a one night stand, Joe."

"That's not what I'm asking you for."

Still, she couldn't make herself say yes.

"Can we do this face to face?" he asked.

"Now?"

"Why not, neither of us is sleeping."

He had that right.

"OK, do—"

A knock sounded at her door. She opened it to find Joe standing there, cell phone in hand.

"I was hoping you wouldn't say no," he said softly, his eyes glowing with passion. He stepped inside and let the door close behind him, shutting out all light and sound so there was just the two of them.

Molly hesitated, not sure what to do, but Joe had no problem finding her in the dark. His hands slid around her waist and he stepped to her. His kisses started at her forehead and with each soft brush of his lips, Molly felt herself relax into him.

He didn't rush. In fact, Molly found herself wishing he would hurry just a little. She ached all over and her heart felt like it was pounding right out of her ribcage.

"You taste so good," Joe murmured.

"Joe," she groaned his name, sliding her hands up to try to anchor herself in the maelstrom of sensations igniting fires in her body. Finally, when she thought she couldn't stand the torture anymore, he captured her lips with his, plying her senses and intoxicating her.

Molly thought she didn't need anything more in life than to be kissed by Joe. Every nerve ending tingled as his lips caressed hers. How could she be so turned on from just a kiss?

And then she quit thinking at all as he lowered her to the bed and followed her down.

Molly cried at the exquisite tenderness he showed her. She cried for all the lost years and all the times she had wanted her husband to touch her – not for sex but in companionship or comfort. Usually all she got was a perfunctory kiss goodbye in the morning and a single kiss goodnight before he rolled over and fell asleep while her body still ached to be held close.

Joe showered her with passion. Not the fiery passion of youth but rather the slow burning ecstasy that comes with living and learning. He quieted her in the aftermath with soft kisses and gentle caresses, whispering adoring things that she wanted desperately to believe.

As early morning light crept across the bed she tried to cover up. "No one except my husband has ever seen me completely naked," she whispered when he wouldn't let her pull the sheet up. Two children and more recently just not caring had taken its toll on her muscle tone and tummy.

"You're beautiful," he told her, smoothing a hand across her belly and then ever so slowly upward to cup her breast. "Don't you know that the intriguing part of a woman is what's inside? A man's a fool if he only looks at the outside wrapping. No one I know can hold a candle to the kind of person you are."

"How did you get so wise?" Molly wound her arms around his neck, pulling him down to meet her kiss.

"A hundred years of bad relationships," he said just before he slanted his mouth across hers.

She caressed his back, his shoulders, and felt the scratchy stubble of his unshaved chin against her cheek.

He broke the kiss and stared down at her.

"You certainly don't act like you're that old," she said, giving him a tender smile.

He rolled over, snugging his hips in-between her thighs. She sighed.

"There's nothing like making love to a good woman to keep a man young."

* * *

Joe left her in the morning, promising he would see her again that night. She knew he was a working man, but still wished he could stay with her. He was two years older than her, she had discovered, but he made her feel like a young girl again. It wasn't just the sex, although that had been more than thoroughly satisfying.

He had listened to her talk about her plans for the mansion, how she was anxious to meet the restoration contractor she had hired by his references and web site only. He had smiled and told her he only hoped the man lived up to her expectations.

From what she had seen of the work being done, it far exceeded her original plans, and yet the statements she had gotten so far were well within the construction estimates he had given her.

She dressed for the day in a filmy skirt and sleeveless sweater. She would have to get herself some period clothes, she thought, as she made her way down the hallway to the business office.

"Has our contractor been in yet this morning?" she asked Tracy.

"No, but then we don't always see him. The crew just starts early and works late."

"Hmm, I wanted to discuss an idea I had last night." She thought about the things Joe had told her. He seemed to know quite a lot about the history of the place and questioned whether the house might contain tunnels from the days of the Underground Railroad. They had brainstormed together and he had finally suggested that if there were tunnels, perhaps they could be restored and expanded into shops

47

or cozy rendezvous nooks for couples wanting to linger over a glass of wine. For a man who professed only having bad relationships, she thought Joe was certainly romantic.

She found some of the men in the ballroom, sanding the hardwood floor that had been discovered beneath the carpet. Little had needed done to it before a new finish was applied, and it was looking beautiful.

"Hello, could you tell me where your boss is working?"

"Said he had some things to do and should be back by lunch," one of the young crewmen said.

Molly had to content herself spending the morning working on the plans for the costume ball. Not finding Mr. Mallory after lunch, she called the office number she had for him but could only leave a message when he didn't answer.

Joe met her at seven, a single rose in hand, and her heart melted a little more. After dinner, they took a walk in the gardens.

"Did you tell your contractor about the tunnels?"

"No, I never saw him. I would think he's a figment of my imagination if not for the fantastic work he's doing."

"I hear he's the best," he replied, stopping on the path and turning to face her.

She let him pull her into the shelter of his arms, enjoying the warmth of his big body.

"Well, he may be the best at restoration, but there's other things a person has to take into consideration." She breathed in his spicy aftershave, touched his cheek before tracing his lips with a finger.

"Oh yeah? Like what?" He nipped her finger then sucked it into his mouth. Molly's stomach felt like a hundred butterflies had taken flight.

"Like kisses that make me tingle clear down to my toes."

"Like this?" He whispered as he sealed her lips with his.

* * *

After seven days of watching the construction progress and as many nights of tender romance and candle light dinners with Joe, Molly decided she quite liked Maple Manor. Well, perhaps it was more Joe's attention that had begun to make her feel so at home.

He was tender and gentle when he made love to her. For the first time in her life, she felt satisfied and fulfilled sexually, but more than that, she was content with her body. He continually told her how attractive he found her and how wonderful she was.

While making love with Joe filled her nights, he also lavished attention on her as they spent time exploring the local history. He was attentive and listened to her opinion even if he adamantly disagreed with her. He touched her often; maybe just a hand at her back or brushing deliberately against her as they walked. When they strolled around town or stood looking at the river, he would lean close and kiss her, sometimes light and brief, but more often long and deep, wrapping his arms around her and pulling her close against him. He was unfailingly polite, but probably the trait she loved the best was his sense of humor and his laugh, which he did often.

"Life is too short to go through it in a bad mood," he told her one night when she asked him why he laughed so much.

She was consulting with the interior decorator one day when Joe walked up behind her, wrapping an arm around her waist. In his hand was a bouquet of flowers.

"These look suspiciously like the flowers from my garden," she said.

He scrunched his lips up at the corner in a way Molly had come to understand meant he was thinking.

"The florist was closed," he finally said.

"In the middle of the day?"

"OK, so I was in a hurry to see you and forgot to stop."

Tracy coughed. The interior decorator laughed. Molly could feel her cheeks warm with a blush.

"Sorry ladies, this is—"

"Call me Joe," he interrupted, putting out his hand and giving both women a wink.

Tracy looked from Joe to Molly with a question in her eyes. She was from the area and Molly wondered if she knew something about Joe that Molly didn't. Even though they spent a lot of time talking, Molly really couldn't say she knew everything about him.

"I, uh, think I've seen you around," Flo, the decorator, said to Joe.

"I've been hanging around a lot," Joe answered.

He was still snuggled up against Molly's back, and she wasn't sure whether to be embarrassed or not. It was such a new experience to have a man shower attention on her like Joe did.

"Can you get away?" He whispered in her ear.

"Don't you have to work?" She turned to ask him. "In fact, what exactly do you do anyway? You never have said."

Tracy began coughing again.

"Are you all right?" Molly asked. Her office manager raised her eyebrows, her eyes watering, hand to mouth. She nodded, unable to speak.

"Come on, I brought a picnic." Joe took her hand and pulled her towards the door. "She'll be back later, ladies." He grinned at the women.

Flo gave him the strangest look Molly had ever seen.

"What was that all about?" She asked as they walked down the hall.

Joe shrugged, "They're probably just jealous because they want my body and you've got it."

She laughed. "Oh, I'm sure that's it."

"Well, damn," he said when they got to the door. "It's raining and I planned a picnic."

Molly clutched her flowers tighter. She probably should have left them in the office in a vase of water. How long had it been since she had been given flowers? Maybe for her birthday years ago because it had saved her husband from having to think about what she liked.

She looked at Joe. For all the gray in his hair and the laugh lines on his tanned face, he looked out at the rain as disappointed as a little boy.

She turned around, grabbing his hand. "Come on. I know where we can go." She led the way, inserting a key in a door and pulling him inside, locking it behind them.

"One of the perks of being the owner," she said with a grin.

Lightning flashed outside the floor to ceiling windows and rain pounded against the glass.

"This is my favorite room so far," she said, turning one of the lamps up just enough to set a glow to the rich interior. "It was the morning room, and we'll use it as a breakfast room once we're officially opened. Mr. Mallory did such a beautiful job restoring it. One of these days if I ever meet the man, I just might tell him."

The door and windows were trimmed with dark wood that matched the mantel and sideboards. Small tables were set in one section, but the half she led Joe to had sofas, low polished tables and a fainting couch, arranged artfully in front of a fireplace.

"Do you want me to light a fire?" Joe asked.

"That would be wonderful. The rain makes it a little chilly." She watched him kneel down, enjoying the view of tight jeans stretching across his buttocks, his shirt snug against his back. Regardless of the nudity so prevalent in the media today, she thought a man actually looked sexier when dressed. There was something sensual and alluring about wondering what was beneath the clothes.

Joe turned and caught her staring.

"What?"

She smiled. "I was just thinking about how sexy you look and how resourceful you are -- bringing me food, building a fire and being so…male."

He grinned. "Come here, Molly Bonner, and I'll show you just how male I can be."

She sat down on the rug beside him. He pulled a bottle of wine, paper cups and some cheese and crackers from his bag.

"A bottle of wine, cheese, and a lovely woman – the basic needs of a man."

She shook her head at him. "For saying all you've had are bad relationships, you are truly a romantic."

He poured some wine and handed her the cup. "Maybe I learned something along the way."

Firelight reflected in his blue eyes as he looked at her. In just a few short days, she had come to anticipate seeing him like a college girl in the first throes of passion. She enjoyed his humor, appreciated his interest in history, and loved the way he looked at her. Given the negative turn her life had taken before she moved to River Bluff, he seemed almost too good to be true. What did a man like Joe see in her? Self-doubts surfaced.

"Joe?"

He leaned close, putting a finger to her lips. As though reading her mind, he said, "You are so lovely. The firelight glints off your hair turning it to burnished gold. I love the way your whole face lights up when you get excited and how you move with such grace." He replaced his finger with his lips, brushing lightly back and forth. "But I especially like the way you kiss me with your whole body."

He took the forgotten cup of wine from her hand, setting it on the stone hearth. His hand came up to her neck, pulling her close.

"You can forget the wine and cheese. All this man needs is one particular woman." He tilted her back gently to the carpet and followed her down, showing her exactly what he meant when he said kissing involved her whole body.

* * *

Even with the strange absence of the contracting foreman every time Molly went looking for him, the progress on the inn was phenomenal. Tracy was already booking guests and events. Molly was busy with the ball, and seeing Joe at night was becoming more important than cornering Mr. Mallory.

In fact, Joe was becoming addictive. Molly kept telling herself it was an adventure and when it was over she would be a better person from having known Joe. But as every day ended lovingly in his arms, she found herself wishing that this particular adventure would never end.

In the meantime, she and Joe actually did discover the entrance to tunnels – behind an old bookcase, no less, like something straight out of a novel. Even though the wood supports and rough flooring were dank and dirty, Molly was now even more anxious to talk to Mallory to see what could be done.

More than a week later, as she finished getting dressed for her date with Joe, someone knocked on her door. The young workman she had spoken to weeks ago stood there with a funny grin on his face.

"Mr. Mallory wants to know if you can come see something he found."

So, the illusive Mr. Mallory finally deigned to meet her. Why now, when she was going to see Joe?

"Do I have to go right now?"

"Well, yes, right now."

"Please," he added when she hesitated.

She suddenly realized she didn't know how to get hold of Joe. He had always just said he lived nearby and he always came to see her at Maple Manor. She had never needed to call him.

And she really did need to see Mr. Mallory, who didn't return her phone calls and was never around when she went looking for him.

"Let me leave a note." She turned back into the room.

"Oh, you don't need, uh, that is, yeah, a note would be fine."

She frowned at the young man's strange comment, but he was looking down the hall so she couldn't read his face.

She followed him to the library where he opened the bookcase to reveal the secret passage. So, Mr. Mallory did know about the tunnels. She thought it was her and Joe's secret.

"Right this way, ma'am."

She stepped passed him when he moved to the side and set a lantern on the floor. An instant later the bookcase swung shut.

"Hey! What's going on?" She started to shout, turning quickly around. She lifted the small lantern to search the wall that led to the library. When she and Joe had ventured down here, she had been behind him when he re-opened the secret door. She never thought to see exactly what he pushed. Now, she was glad she had written a note stating she was seeing Mr. Mallory. Joe would come looking for her.

She turned carefully, holding the lantern so she could see the set of steps not far from the entrance. It was then she noticed light past the first curve in the tunnel. Cautiously she stepped down, following the small arc of light she held in front of her.

"Hello, anyone here?"

No answer.

She felt her way along the narrow passage, which gradually turned to where she knew there were two small rooms across from each other. She and Joe figured they had probably been storerooms along with being used to hide runaway slaves.

She gasped when she turned into the room filled with light. Candles sat in wrought iron sconces on creamy textured walls. A striped sofa was against the wall, gold and maroon matching pillows giving the room a warm atmosphere. Vintage hunting pictures graced the walls and a burnished wood commode, complete with pitcher and bowl, was positioned near the door. In the center stood a walnut table, already set with elegant china, silver and crystal. A bottle of wine stood chilling in a silver bucket.

She could only think that Mr. Mallory was responsible, but how had he known what she and Joe had discussed, or that she had dreamed of just such an elegant, romantic hideaway?

"Mr. Mallory?" She called to him. Regardless of the beauty surrounding her, it was a little disconcerting to be down here alone.

"Ms Bonner."

She spun around at the sound of his voice and thought she was looking at a ghost from the past.

"Joe?"

He wore a cutaway coat of dark brown, buff knee breeches and high-topped boots. A white shirt beneath a gold embroidered vest was topped with a flowing cravat.

"How?" She was speechless, and he just stood there smiling at her. "How did the contractor know what we talked about?"

Joe bowed, taking her hand and planting a kiss on her wrist. "Joseph Mallory Austin, historical preservationist." He lifted his head, adding, "I inherited the company from my maternal grandfather, Patrick Mallory."

"It was you all the time?" she asked. "Why didn't you say something?" Before he could answer, she added, "You never returned my phone calls!"

He shrugged, grinning sheepishly. "I wanted to surprise you."

"Well, you certainly did that. It's beautiful – more wonderful than I had imagined."

Suddenly all the knowing smiles and strange comments made sense.

"Everyone knows."

He nodded. "When I first met you, I didn't know you were the owner. Then I wanted to see how you liked my work without being influenced because of our relationship. The deeper we became involved, the harder it was to own up to the truth. Don't be mad at Tracy. I made her promise not to tell you."

She just shook her head at him. "Are you keeping any more secrets from me?"

"Just one, but first tell me what you think of this."

He took her hand and pulled her over to where a sideboard took up most of the wall. "Look."

He pushed a button and she heard a motor whirl. In just minutes, the picture above the sideboard slid up revealing a dumbwaiter, on which were several covered dishes.

"Your couples can order dinner before they come down," he said as he lifted the platters out onto the sideboard. "Then it's served, via our silent waiter, and they are not disturbed by people coming in and out."

"And why wouldn't they want to be disturbed?" she asked the question, already having a pretty good idea of the answer.

He circled her waist and pulled her close, giving her a kiss that lingered until her knees went weak.

"Because they may have other things in mind to do, along with eating, that is."

"Oh," was all she could say.

He led her over to the sofa. She sank down onto the softness, lying back against the pillows.

"What do you think?"

"First, I want to know what your other secret is." She looked up at him.

He dropped onto one knee beside the sofa. "I've fallen in love with you," he softly whispered.

She knew her heart was shining in her eyes as she replied. "In that case, I think this particular part of the mansion is not going to be open to the public." She opened her arms and he came to her, his laughter filling her heart with love.

Magnolia Summer

North of Nashville, 1866

Thomas Remington remembered Richelle Farnsworth as a happy little girl with braids who had followed her brother, Peter, and him around like a shadow. Of course, that had been eight years ago – before the war and before Peter had died. And even though he had seen her at the funeral, by that time he had hardened his heart until all he thought about was revenge.

He watched her now as she descended the curved stairway for her eighteenth birthday party and his breath caught at her beauty. She was dainty and soft spoken, and the scent of magnolias reached him where he stood in the shadows. She spoke to each person who greeted her with birthday felicitations, her smile never faltering and her responses genuine.

As the night wore on, he realized there was more substance to her than most other women he knew in Nashville. Her eyes sparkled with wisdom yet her mouth curved upward with just a hint of humor. She was the epitome of all things gentle and southern, and she reminded him of what he had missed during the war and of everything he had lost. He was strongly drawn to her, his body throbbing in reply to each smile she gave another. He hadn't expected to actually like Richelle Farnsworth, and that made his mission all the harder.

* * *

The night was magical, and Richelle felt quite elegant in her new ball gown and upswept hair, both styled to show the world she had reached maturity and should be taken seriously as a woman. As she danced with gentleman after gentleman, mostly friends of her distant cousin, James, she evaluated them as potential suitors. The war was over, and she was determined to carry on -- to marry and have a family.

She had no experience to speak of, for all the eligible men in the county had been to war for the past several years. That had left the young stable hands, who had been more than willing to experiment with her, but their wet kisses and heavy petting had added little to her education.

Even with those thoughts in mind, she felt nothing toward the men who held her gently and politely waltzed her around the ballroom.

Richelle felt sure there should be a spark of some kind when they touched; a glimmer of danger in their eyes when they gazed at her; a physical throbbing in her loins as when she touched herself in the dark of night.

"Richelle, will you honor me with this dance?" James didn't wait for an answer but swept her into his arms and out onto the dance floor. "You look ravishing," he said, pulling her closer than was proper.

When she looked up at him, his gaze was glued to her bosom, his lips a smirk. She didn't care for her cousin. He had moved in with them at Farnsworth Hollow years ago, and from the time Richelle had turned sixteen, he had pursued her with a single-minded purpose. Now, she tried to put some distance between them without causing a scene, but he squeezed her hand in warning.

"You know what is to happen, cousin. And if you do not smile sweetly and appear happy with your prospects, you shall never set foot on your precious Hollow again." Before she could ask his meaning, he stopped dancing and tugged her toward the front of the ballroom. A curt chop of his hand silenced the musicians.

"My dear friends. I am most pleased to announce that Richelle has agreed to become my wife."

Richelle tried to tug her hand free; to deny his claim and leave, but James twisted her arm behind her back and jerked it upward to the point of pain. To anyone looking on, it would appear from the front an embrace; a show of affection. Richelle knew better.

"We will, of course, be married as soon as possible and reside here on Richelle's beloved Farnsworth Hollow."

Polite applause greeted his announcement and his friends immediately surrounded them. In the midst of the camaraderie she managed to pry his arm from around her and slip away. He knew she would not go far. After all, the Hollow had been her home all her life and with no family left, she had nowhere to go.

She breathed deeply as she hurried along the outside patio, stepping lightly down the stone path and moving toward the gazebo at the other end of the garden. The summer air was heavy, as though a storm was imminent, and the rich scent of magnolias was everywhere. Normally Richelle loved the summer months. The days were unbearably hot, but the flower gardens were in full bloom, the foals romped in the pastures, and the fields were fertile with crops.

Tonight, however, she noticed none of the splendor of her home as she hung her head, tears silently falling into her lap. Oh, how she missed her father and brother. If they were here, she wouldn't be forced to marry. It was because they had died in the war that James would inherit the Hollow, and the only way she could remain a part of it was to marry him. She shivered in repulsion.

A sound in the shadows of the trees caused Richelle to straighten, though she was not afraid. She knew every inch of the plantation and all who lived here. Still, she watched carefully as a darker shape detached itself from the night gloom and came toward her.

"I have watched you grow from an inquisitive and mischievous child into a beautiful woman," a man said as he leaned a broad shoulder against one pillar of the gazebo, crossing his arms over his chest. His voice, smooth as the richest velvet, touched a chord deep within her that was scary and exciting all at the same time.

The moonlight made his hair shine gold, but then clouds bedeviled her view and she could not clearly see his face. It mattered not, for she knew it was Thom, her brother's best friend, and though Richelle had not seen him for three years – since Peter's funeral -- she had loved him since she was ten years old.

"I promised your brother and father I would look after you as though you were my own sister," he continued as he stepped into the gazebo, the sound of his boot heels not as loud as Richelle's rapidly beating heart. "But seeing you here, like an angel gracing our humble midst, I find my thoughts are anything but brotherly."

Her breath caught at his words, innately knowing he wanted something more from her than conversation. She put out a hand to touch him and he pulled her to her feet and into his arms.

Thomas wrapped his arms around Richelle and bent his head to her lips. He kissed her hungrily, ravishing her mouth and forcing her lips apart to delve deeper. Keeping her securely anchored against him with one arm, he stroked her shoulder, sliding the puffed sleeve of her gown down her arm. Roughly his hand cupped her bared breast, squeezing and molding it to fit his palm.

To think, he had actually stepped forward in the ballroom to request a dance from Richelle, thinking she would welcome a visit from him. That was right before she stood beside his enemy and announced her intention to marry him. Now, Thomas thought, what better way to extract retribution against James than to bury himself in his betrothed and take her virginity. Ah, that would be the ultimate revenge.

He twisted about and sat, pulling Richelle onto his lap. Taking both her hands in a gentle grip behind her back, he kissed her again, sucking her tongue into his mouth then following it back to hers in a duel for control. He gathered her skirts up, sliding his hand along her bare leg to her knee. He left her sweet mouth to kiss a heated trail down her throat to her breast. She was so soft; her skin like the finest silk. He laved her nipple with his tongue, nipping the rigid peak before sucking.

His hand skimmed over the ruffled edge of her pantalets, higher until he insinuated it between her tightly clasped legs. He could feel her heat through the cotton and it spurred him on.

"Open for me," he whispered against her breast, then sucked harder on the outer softness, wanting to leave his mark on her skin so James would know she had been with another.

"Thom," she cried softly, tugging against the hold he had on her wrists even as she spread her legs to allow him to touch her through the slit in her drawers. And his name on her lips was his undoing, for he realized he could not exact his revenge on Richelle. His honor demanded he watch over her but as her womanly scent reached his nostrils, he knew he would have to finish what he had started, albeit leaving her innocence somewhat intact.

He released her hands and she immediately wrapped her arms around his neck, lifting her face for his kiss. His mouth swallowed her cry as he speared her with his fingers, feeling the heat and wetness of her feminine core. She stiffened at the onset but then moved against his fingers as though wanting more, urging him to deepen his strokes. He slid his thumb along her curls before finding the hidden pearl of her sex. Stroking her lightly and then deeper, he brought her to climax. He fleetingly wondered if she had already taken James for a lover but at this point knew it would make no difference. He slid his hand down, released her from his kiss and set her on the bench. Even though he ached from unfulfilled lust, he steeled his voice to speak.

"Think of this on your wedding night, sweet Richelle. You will be in the arms of another but you will remember how this felt; how I made you ache and cry out in ecstasy."

"But I never—" Richelle couldn't finish. She watched as he faded back into the dark and silent night.

* * *

"You will set a wedding date before this week is out," James shouted at her across the space of the table and Richelle flinched at his tone. He had insinuated himself into their family years ago, but as long as her father or Peter had been in residence, his tone had always been cajoling and docile. How had Richelle ever thought him a gentleman?

When she didn't answer, James threw his napkin on the table and stormed to where she sat. He grabbed her chin, forcing her to look at him.

"If you do not do as I say, perhaps I shall marry another, and you will be forced to leave your beloved horse farm, forever."

"I do not love you," she replied, her gaze meeting his cold, flinty stare.

He laughed. "Love has nothing to do with it, my dear. But if you continue to thwart me, I shall have to fuck you; perhaps even get you with child, and then you will have no choice." He bent close, his breath sour against her cheek. His finger traced the swell of her bosom above the ruffle on her dress and Richelle shivered in loathing.

"In fact, perhaps I should fuck you anyway, just to teach you a lesson." His hand cupped her breast and squeezed painfully.

Richelle swung her foot out, kicking him in the shin and surprising him so he loosened his hold. She quickly stood and moved to the other side of the table, grabbing the servant bell and ringing it quickly. Solomon entered immediately. If there was one thing Richelle had learned about James in the time he had been there, it was that appearances were everything. He would never make a scene, even in front of servants.

"You rang, Miss." Solomon's voice was not in the least submissive, and Richelle felt better knowing that the servant, who had been with her family forever, somehow felt the unpleasant undercurrents.

"We are through here, Solomon." Richelle spoke to him, but her gaze never left James and she hoped he understood the words were actually directed at him.

⁕ ⁕ ⁕

Richelle awoke, heart racing and gown damp and clinging to her skin. Her body throbbed with unfulfilled passion and she could only think she had once again been dreaming of Thom. Her hands skimmed over her breasts, the tips rigid and aching, the cotton of her gown abrading them. As her palms slid further down her body, she closed her eyes on a sigh, wanting to feel again the pressure of his fingers, the touch of his hot breath on her skin.

With a dainty curse she swung her feet over the side of the bed and stood, knowing no amount of touching could give her the same pleasure that Thom had on that single night in the glen. He had certainly been right when he said she would recall it, for not a night went by that she didn't want him with an aching intensity. She wandered out on the balcony, hoping a breeze would cool her fevered skin. A quarter moon cast shadows across the lawn and she searched the darkness, hoping he would emerge and come to her.

Thomas Remington's family had owned the land next to the Hollow, and when his parents had died in an accident when he was young, her father had purchased Misty Valley to hold it in trust for Thom. In the meantime, Thom had become part of their family, and he and Peter had been best friends. Richelle had tagged along behind them, riding her pony after them as they galloped across the pastures. She had even hidden in the hayloft the day they had taken two dairymaids up to the hay. At ten years of age, she hadn't understood what was happening, but she had secretly given her young heart to the handsome eighteen year old.

By the time she was old enough to understand what her body craved, the war came and both Peter and Thomas were called to serve the cause. Her father felt duty bound also, and by the time it was all said and done, she had lost them both. Only Thomas had returned unharmed, and when he came to the funeral, so achingly handsome in his uniform, Richelle had thrown herself at him, begging him to take her with him when he left.

He had refused, perhaps because the war was not over, or because Richelle had only been fifteen and Thomas was a gentleman through and through. Whatever the reason, he had kissed her gently on the forehead and left her again; her young heart grieving for her loss and for something she could not name.

Now, that same sense of need stole over her as she silently traversed the stairs from the balcony and wandered across the lawn. The damp grass felt cool against her bare feet, the slight breeze welcome in the sultry summer night. When she reached the gazebo, she turned back towards her home, a dark silhouette against the wavering light of the moon. She ached for everything that might have been; for she knew in her heart she could never marry James, even if it meant losing Farnsworth Hollow forever.

Richelle sat in the gazebo, the air heavy and oppressive, and her skin hot even though she wore only a thin cotton nightgown. It was only slightly cooler in the night, for the summer was at its zenith, when the fields begged for a drop of moisture and the heat rose in lazy waves from the landscape when the sun blazed down at the height of the day.

She remained quiet, hoping that if she waited long enough -- wished hard enough -- that he would come to her again. It had been seven nights, eight if she counted this one, since her birthday ball and not a day had passed when she didn't think of him. Alone in her bed at night, she would allow her hands to wander the path his had taken, pleasuring herself as he had done. But it was not the same without the heat of his kisses. Even the brand he had left on her skin had faded and she longed for him to come to her again.

She was drawn from her thoughts when she felt his presence. The glade was utterly still, as though holding its breath for something momentous to occur. She tried to still her racing heart.

He stepped closer, taking her hands and drawing her gently to her feet. Richelle caught the glint of mystery in his gaze, his tawny eyes reflecting the moonlight. His movements reminded her of a jungle cat – a predator -- far more dangerous than she had imagined. She tried to pull back but his grip was firm. And then it was too late.

* * *

Without thought of discovery, Thomas swept his black cloak around Richelle, completely blanketing her pale gown and hair before lifting her in his arms. Long strides took him swiftly across the manicured grounds, into the trees and away from the light spilling from the Farnsworth Mansion. The bundle in his arms was featherweight, and even though she struggled to free herself, Thomas had no problem holding her securely. He did, however, have a problem keeping his mind on the matter at hand for her soft curves made him ache.

"Let me go!" Her voice was muffled, and each wiggle against him heated his blood. Without answering her, he lifted her into the boat, signaling quietly for his oarsman to shove off and row the skiff around the bend to where his schooner sat at anchor in the wide Cumberland River.

Not until he had her safely aboard the Revenge did he dare set her down and uncover her head, securing the clasp of his cloak at her throat. It took only a moment for her to get her bearings, but before she could scream he placed his hand over her mouth.

"Not only will no one come to your aid, fair Richelle, but I do not need the noise to compound the headache I already have this eve."

He gazed into her emerald eyes where tears threatened to spill down her pale cheeks. She said but one word when he removed his hand.

"Why?"

Thomas felt the boat move beneath him and braced his booted feet to take the sway. He griped the railing on either side of her to steady her as they began to move downstream. Only then did he answer her. "I'm honor bound to watch over you."

"I would have come to you on your word alone. You would not have had to steal me from my home." She squared her shoulders and Thomas wondered if he'd have a fight on his hands. He almost hoped so, for it would somehow absolve him from guilt for having taken her for his own purposes. "This is how you honor my father's request?"

Thomas Remington sighed, running his fingers through his hair, not realizing what it did to Richelle's emotions. Even though she was being kidnapped from the only home she'd ever had, she wasn't frightened. After all, this was Thomas, and deep in her heart she loved him.

"It is complicated."

She touched his cheek, loving the feel of smooth, taut skin. His eyes were haunted, and she ached to take away the hurt she saw there. She turned and reached for his hand, leading him down the stairs, along the narrow corridor to what she assumed was the Captain's cabin – his cabin. She didn't speak until she had closed the door behind her.

She turned to face him, dropping his cloak from her shoulders. "Then help me understand."

The light from the cabin lantern glowed behind Richelle, making her nightgown transparent and highlighting lush curves. Thomas knew he was lost as he gathered her in his arms.

"Not a night has gone by when I don't dream of you," he whispered raggedly as he feathered kisses across her face. "I should never have touched you that night, for now I ache for what I cannot have."

"I know there is more than what we shared. Teach me to please you, Thom." Her hands were everywhere as she spoke, pulling his shirt from his breeches, skimming her palms along the muscles of his back.

Thomas groaned. "You are promised to another—"

"I do not want to marry James!" She pushed against him and he let her go, hoping the distance would calm the fires raging within him. "I never agreed to marry him. The announcement he made was without my knowledge."

"You did not refute it."

"I am doing so now, to the only person who matters to me."

As he watched, she reached down and grabbed the hem of her gown, pulling it up and off. Thomas's breath caught. She stood straight and proud, her breasts firm, her slim waist and the flair of her hips causing his palms to itch.

"I want only you." Her words crashed over him as a ship on a rocky shore, breaking his defenses and washing away his anger.

She came to him, her dainty fingers gathering his shirt and tugging it over his head, and still he could only stand there, gazing at her beauty. She wrapped her arms around his neck, brushing her breasts against his chest.

With a growl, Thomas swept her into his arms and carried her to the bed. Her eyes gazed trustingly up at him as he stripped the rest of his clothes.

When Thom stood before her, gloriously naked, Richelle's heart beat so hard she thought it would burst from her chest. Where she had once compared him to a jungle predator, she now thought him more like the stallions that raced after the mares. He was certainly hung like one, and she couldn't stop herself from reaching out for him. She knew nothing about pleasuring a man; instinct alone guided her as she caressed him. That and Thom's quivering hips and the groan she heard as she leaned over and kissed the tip of him.

He threaded his fingers through her hair, urging her on, and Richelle felt her own ache build as she continued to caress him.

"Enough," Thom growled, gently removing her hands before lying down beside her. His lips found hers and Richelle could feel the hunger in the forceful way he invaded her mouth -- tongue exploring, enticing her to taste him. She forgot to breathe as his hand skimmed her shoulder then her breast.

She squirmed restlessly as he caressed her for a mere second before sliding down, over her hip to the juncture of her legs. He didn't have to ask this time, for Richelle bent one leg, opening herself to his explorations. She was aching and needed what she knew Thom could give her.

He rolled her onto her back, settling his hips between her legs. She could feel the hot length of him against her thigh and her own temperature rose. When he released her mouth from his drugging kisses, she breathed rapidly, feeling panic rise in her chest.

"There will be no going back." Thom moved his hips forward and back and she could feel him probing her feminine opening. "Is this what you want?"

She spread her legs, raising her knees and he settled more heavily against her hips. "I want you," she whispered as she circled his neck with her arms.

Her wetness and scent were enough to drive any man insane, and Thomas knew he couldn't stop, even though honor demanded he make sure he had Richelle's permission. When she opened more fully to him, he was lost. He reached down and positioned himself, knowing he would have to go slow for her to take his length. He rubbed the secret button of her sex as he pushed forward, slid back and then forward again, a little deeper this time.

Richelle locked her legs around his waist, lifting her hips to meet his movements. "More," she breathed huskily, and he pushed forward again, this time breaking through her maidenhead and seating himself deep inside her. She stiffened briefly but did not cry out. Instead, she tightened her legs around him and urged him on.

Thomas rocked forward again and again, the feel of her sending liquid fire through his veins. She took all of him and when he pulled back to the very edge of her, her heels pushed against his buttocks to bring him back deep within her.

"I feel you," she rasped, "in every part of me." And then she gasped in wonder, her eyes locked with his as she climaxed.

Thomas didn't stop, the friction caused by his movements and her orgasm pushing him over the edge. He came in hot, hard spurts, throbbing inside her heat as she continued to squeeze around him, draining him.

His arms quivered as he tried to hold himself up so as not to crush her with his weight, but she tugged him down and so he rolled to the side, bringing her with him. She peppered his chest with kisses, her hand caressing his hot skin. Too sensitized to handle any more, he grabbed her wrist and held it still against his chest.

"I felt you." Her voice held a sense of awe.

He looked down at her and couldn't help but chuckle. "You are not supposed to speak of such things."

"Why not?"

"Well, because fine ladies just..." He didn't know what to say.

"Does it always feel like this?" she asked.

He could only shake his head at her audacity. "I wouldn't know. I'm not a lady."

She gave him a dazzling smile and wiggled her hips against him, causing him to stir to life already. "You certainly aren't. And I am ever so glad of that fact." She pushed against his shoulder and he rolled until she was on top of him. She straightened, sitting tight against his hips, his shaft still embedded deep within her.

"Do you want more?" he asked, his hands sliding up her ribs to cup her breasts.

She covered his hands with her own. "Might I please?" she asked in her most ladylike voice.

* * *

Much later in the morning, Thomas left Richelle sleeping in his berth as he went topside to speak with his first mate. They would head downriver for Nashville where Thomas would set his plan in motion. He grabbed some breakfast in the galley, and then had Cook fix a tray to take back to his cabin. When he entered, he found Richelle brushing her hair, her body only partially covered with one of his shirts. He immediately hardened, his shaft straining against his breeches, his hands gripping the tray to hold it steady. He hadn't realized she would have such an effect on him, and only hoped he could remain steadfast in his plan.

Her face brightened when she saw the tray and promptly sat at his desk, allowing him to serve her. He found he liked the idea of taking care of her, and sat in a chair opposite to watch her eat.

When she finished, she gazed at him over the rim of her coffee cup. "Are you now ready to tell me why you kidnapped me?" Her eyes glittered with humor, and Thomas recalled her comments about coming willingly. Had he known what would transpire when he had her alone, he might have moved his plan up by several months. He closed his eyes briefly, trying to shut out her winsome figure and what they had done last night. He thought instead of James and all that man had cost him.

"Your cousin has claimed all that belonged to your family." His voice hardened as he spoke. He thought crushingly of her father's and Peter's tragic deaths in the horrid war.

"It became his by right of birth."

He frowned. "I don't believe that was what your father would have wanted. Many women now own property, and I'm sure your father would have known the Hollow would be safe in your hands. Yet there is no way to prove it. Be that as it may, Misty Valley was mine, and yet James has claimed that also, for back taxes which he says I did not pay while I was away fighting for his birthright."

Thom's anger was an almost tangible force, and Richelle knew how strongly he felt about the horse-breeding farm he had started on land her father had held in trust for him.

"Perhaps if you allowed me to talk to him--" she began.

"There will be no talk -- unless he agrees to my ransom." He jerked up from the chair, moving to brace his hands on the small porthole, not looking at her.

Richelle's stomach dropped, dreading the question she knew she must ask. "What ransom?" she whispered.

"Misty Valley," he paused, his tone full of regret, "in exchange for you."

"You would do that, after what we have shared?"

Thomas looked over his shoulder. She stood and watched his gaze travel from the deep vee in his shirt where her breasts were clearly visible, down to where her bare legs showed below the hem, which only came to mid-thigh.

He pushed off from the wall, turning toward her with a sigh before giving her a wicked grin. "I fear I must now come up with a different plan."

* * *

Thomas made port in Nashville, giving his men a long awaited furlough. He spirited Richelle to his rented rooms where he hoped to come up with another plan to regain his rights to Misty Valley. Richelle, however, had other ideas. Since he had abducted her without even so much as a petticoat, she could not leave his rooms and so they spent their days and nights exploring each other. Richelle was unquenchable in her thirst for carnal knowledge, and Thomas found himself indulging her every request.

She liked being on top, and at that very moment, rode him like a wild stallion. Thomas bucked beneath her, ramming deep each time she ground her hips against his. He loved watching her changing expressions, which varied from wanton lust to wonder and awe each time she climaxed. She was glorious to look at, her hair in wild disarray, her breasts jiggling with the rhythm of her hips. Her bare skin glistened with a fine sheen of perspiration from the heat, but it hadn't stopped her from wanting him. And it hadn't made Thomas hesitate to take her again and again whether in the heat of the day or the middle of the night.

Her movements increased and he knew she was close.

"Come with me," she rasped, catching and holding his gaze.

He clutched her hips, holding her firm as he felt her come, squeezing around him.

"Yes!" he shouted, pulsing hot and heavy deep into her womb. She collapsed on his chest, her breathing as ragged as his own, and he held her close. He knew now that he loved her, and wanted to spend the remainder of his life with her by his side. But at present, he had nothing to offer her unless he could reclaim his inheritance.

When his breathing had calmed so that he could speak, he asked, "Does James have papers documenting that Farnsworth Hollow became his upon your father's death?"

Richelle lifted her head, propping her chin on stacked fists on his chest. "Must we speak of him?" She made a face when Thomas nodded.

"I have never seen any documents, but then I have never thought to ask. When first Father, and then Peter died," she paused, drawing a shaky breath and Thomas gently stroked her bare back. She continued, "I was beyond despair. By the time I began taking an interest in things, James had fired father's man of business and had taken over the record keeping. He had also replaced the head groom in the horse barn, and had put a different overseer in charge of the fields. I didn't question his right to do so."

"So perhaps the Hollow is actually yours," Thomas mused then sat up so suddenly that Richelle nearly fell off the bed. He grabbed her just in time, sitting her on the comforter as he began to pace the room. "Why else would James be trying so hard to marry you if not to legally claim that which is yours as your husband?"

Richelle scooted up against the headboard, not at all minding the sight before her, for Thom was naked and beautiful to behold. His muscles bunched in his legs, his male member swinging free with his movements. His skin was bronzed from the sun, his dark blonde hair curling wildly about his face. He looked like a pirate, and Richelle was happy to be his booty.

"That's it!" He swung to face her, fists on hips.

"Oh, yes," she said, her gaze on a certain portion of his anatomy, "that most certainly is it."

Thomas tried to concentrate on the matter at hand, which Richelle made quite difficult, given she lay naked on his bed. He had come up with another plan, but he didn't think Richelle would care for it at all. In truth, he didn't like the fact that it would put her in danger, but it was the only way they could put an end to his quest.

* * *

"I will not seduce James!" Richelle shouted at him and Thomas knew his entire crew could hear, even though they stood alone on the bow. He had waited until they were sailing upriver before broaching his plan to her, knowing she would react in just this way.

"You won't have to actually sleep with him," Thomas tried to soothe her. "Just keep

84

him occupied long enough for me to search the study for documents pertaining to ownership of Misty Valley and the Hollow."

"I thought the idea was ransom – me for the land, but once you had the deeds, I just wouldn't show back up at Farnsworth Hollow."

Thomas glanced away, not wanting to hurt Richelle with the truths he had recently learned. However, to obtain her assistance for his new plan, he felt he must.

"Your cousin is telling everyone that you are dead, and to honor your memory and his love for you, he has recently changed the name of the Hollow to Magnolia Mansion because of the beautiful flowers you loved and planted in abundance around the grounds."

"Dead?"

He watched the surprise show on her face, and knew when he told her the rest of it, she would readily agree with his plan. "In reality, he received the ransom note and has refused to part with the acreage and prize thoroughbreds, even in exchange for your life."

"How do you know this?" she asked in a small voice and Thomas could tell she couldn't believe her cousin would stoop so low.

"Solomon sent word through my man."

"That...that bastard," she swore, her eyes narrowing. "I shall try to seduce him if only to get him close enough to kill."

Thomas wrapped her in his arms, chuckling over her vehemence, even as he kissed away her anger. "It will do me no good to regain Misty Valley if you are hanged for murder."

"We are ready, Captain," his first mate interrupted the moment.

Thomas set Richelle away from him. "Can you do this?" He searched her face.

She took a steadying breath. "If I know you will be nearby."

He kissed her quickly. "I would not send you there without knowing I could protect you. Besides, the place will be surrounded by my men, and Solomon knows we are coming."

* * *

Richelle regained her bedroom without being seen and donned fresh clothes before going in search of James. He didn't seem all that surprised when she walked into the study where he sat behind her father's desk.

"Did Remington have no further use for you after I refused to grant his ransom?"

Richelle suppressed a shiver at his evil look. "I managed to escape." She forced herself to smile at him. "You know I would do anything to stay here on my beloved Hollow." Her hips swayed seductively as she ventured closer, still keeping the desk between them.

"You mean you would whore for me?"

She blanched at his words, but forced herself to go on. "I will do whatever it takes."

His eyes narrowed and he got up, walking around the side of the desk towards her. "Perhaps I would be willing to fuck you."

He reached for her so suddenly Richelle didn't have time to retreat. Roughly pulling her against him, James's mouth took hers in a brutal kiss. His hand cupped her breast, squeezing painfully and it was all Richelle could do not to cry out.

"Not here," she managed to say when he released her mouth. "Upstairs."

James savagely pulled her from the room and Richelle had to grab her skirts up to keep from falling. Her heart beat rapidly, her arm bruised from his cruel grip. The only thing that kept her from fighting back was the glimpse she had of Thomas in the shadows as James dragged her up the stairs.

James tossed her onto the bed and turned to lock the door. Richelle quickly regained her footing and moved across the room. When he turned back, already jerking off his coat, she sent a silent prayer for Thomas to hurry.

"Well, let's see if that bastard taught you anything," James smirked, pulling his cravat off and stretching it between his hands as he sauntered toward her. When she didn't move, his eyes narrowed.

"Is this some kind of game?"

Richelle shook her head. "No. I...we don't have to hurry." She moved shaking hands to the buttons at her throat. Oh, God, she couldn't do this. But then she recalled James's deception and her hands stilled.

Ever so slowly, she began undoing her bodice, her eyes never leaving his face. He had divested himself of waistcoat and shirt and when she didn't move fast enough, he cornered her by the window seat, ripping her blouse and chemise to the waist.

She gasped, trying to cover her nakedness, but he twisted her around, slamming her against the wall, pinning her there with his hips.

"You'll fuck me now!" He twisted a hand in her hair, tugging painfully as he grabbed at her skirts with his other hand.

When she felt his hand on her bare thigh, she screamed.

"Thomas!"

James immediately stilled, nostrils flaring, eyes narrowed. "You bitch. I should have known it was a trick." He slapped her and Richelle fell against the window seat. Before she could recover, James had removed a pistol from the drawer by the bed and was hurrying to the door.

"No!" Richelle scrambled to her feet, racing after him. She stopped at the top of the stairs, frozen by the scene before her. She had yelled for Thomas to save her, and he must have heard for he was part way up the staircase, a cluster of documents in one hand. James stood two steps below her, his pistol leveled at Thomas's chest.

Richelle bit her lip to keep from crying out.

"So, you have found out my little secret," James spoke with a sneer. "I was here for years, taking care of everything while you and Peter and the old man were off seeking glory in a war I knew was hopeless. And yet you were to have Misty Valley and he left me nothing!" His voice rose as he yelled at Thom and Richelle could see the pistol waver in his shaking hand.

James gave an evil laugh. "I was even willing to marry the bitch to keep it all legally." At his slur, Thomas growled and moved up a step. James steadied his hand. "But you got to her first, and I will never take your leavings."

The click of his pistol being cocked spurred Richelle into action. She stepped forward and shoved him in the back as hard as she could. The pistol discharged as he tumbled down the stairs and she saw Thom fall against the wall.

"No, oh, God, please no," she cried, rushing down the remaining stairs, carefully stepping around James's still form. She crouched beside Thom, her trembling hands touching him everywhere, looking for wounds.

"Do I have to be bleeding for you to continue this attention?" Thomas asked as he circled her arms, settling her on his lap.

"You're not hurt?" she asked, her hand on his arm, her gaze searching his face. It was then that Thomas noticed the bruise on her cheek and her torn dress. He might have to kill James if he wasn't already dead. He dipped his head for a kiss before he heard footsteps running from the rear of the mansion. Quickly he removed his coat and wrapped it around Richelle's shoulders, protecting her from the servants' view.

Shotgun in hand, Solomon cautiously approached James, but the man didn't move. Thomas helped Richelle to her feet, keeping himself between her and James. She clung to him, refusing to let him move from her side to investigate. He had to smile, wondering who was protecting whom.

"Is he...?" she began, and Thomas hoped she had not killed James. For even if it had been an accident and thoroughly justified, he did not want a killing to weigh on her conscience.

Just then James groaned, but when he tried to sit up, Solomon put a booted foot to his back and held him down on the floor. The servant looked over at Thomas. "Never did care for that man, no siree."

Thomas grinned. "Have the men take him out to the stables and secure him in the tack room. We'll have him transferred to Nashville for trial as soon as we can notify the authorities."

He turned and scooped Richelle into his arms. "Have someone bring water up for a bath and some food." He started up the stairs as he spoke and Richelle circled his neck, snuggling close. "And tell everyone Miss Farnsworth is not to be disturbed." He could feel her kiss his neck, his skin instantly heating beneath her lips.

"Yes, sir," Solomon said, and Thomas didn't have to look behind him to know the servant was smiling.

* * *

"Don't leave me," Richelle begged when he put her down beside the tub of hot water. "I was so afraid he had shot you; that I had caused your death." She clung to his neck and Thomas rubbed her back, murmuring soothing words close to her ear. Gradually she quit shaking and began to return his caresses, her hands sliding down his back to his buttocks.

"Love me." She rained hot kisses on his neck, up his chin to his face. "Make me forget his touch."

Thomas growled, recalling her torn bodice. Had he gotten to her too late?

He set her away from him, but she refused to be still. Her hands divested him of his shirt, and then skimmed down his bare torso to the fastener on his breeches. As he yanked his boots off, she stripped off her dress and underclothes until she stood gloriously naked before him.

She took his hand and stepped into the tub, letting him settle into the water before she sat down in his lap, sighing as she relaxed against him. The warm, fragrant water smelled of magnolias, which would forever remind Thomas of her. She took the hand she held and placed it over her breast, but Thomas needed no urging to take what she offered.

He caressed her breasts, then lower where his fingers found her heat. She arched against him, pushing her soft derriere against him.

"Now," she demanded, moving her feet to the outside of his thighs, opening herself to him. She caressed his length before positioning herself so he could slide into her.

Thomas smiled as she sighed. Richelle was a woman to be reckoned with, but he didn't mind giving her what she wanted, for pleasuring her insured an equal amount of ecstasy for him.

Most of the bath water had been splashed onto the floor by the time Richelle cried out in rapture and Thomas groaned as she squeezed around him, rapidly following her climax with one of his own. He cradled her in his arms, content with his life, until she began shivering with cold. Only after he had toweled them both off and tucked her beside him in her bed did he think about the documents he had found in the study.

He propped himself up on his elbow, turning toward Richelle. She lazily opened her eyes when he began a slow caress of her satin skin.

"I did find the documents we needed in your father's study."

Her eyes widened. "And does James really own the Hollow and Misty Valley?"

He shook his head. "I can't believe he actually kept papers which clearly show

Farnsworth Hollow belongs to you, to be held in trust by your husband if you marry before you turn twenty-five; otherwise it is yours free and clear. I suspect he thought to marry you, secure the trust, and then either get you to sign the land over to him, or kill you."

She shivered and he bent to kiss her, sharing his heat and his love.

"What about Misty Valley?" She curled her fingers into his hair. He could feel her heart beat beneath his lips as he kissed the soft skin there before he answered.

"There were also papers from your father stating the taxes and arrears to Misty Valley were paid in full before he left here and that property shall remain mine, or my descendants." He rolled over and slid between her thighs, hungry again for what only she could give him. "Or our descendants, if you are willing to share my life."

She laughed delightfully, opening herself to him. Thomas realized that revenge was a useless emotion, and he would be better served if he spent his time loving Richelle and making a life with her. For although property and material possessions may be necessary to sustain life, they could never compare to the warmth of her smile, or the sharing of laughter and love.

The Philosophy of Love

Dried leaves crunched beneath her combat boots as Mert hunched over, trying to keep the chilly wind from seeping down her neck. It would be too cold to sleep in the park tonight, especially with no more than her light coat. She had exactly fifty-two dollars and thirty-eight cents left to her name and that wasn't even enough for a hotel. Damn Stu for locking her out of her apartment, even if she was behind on the rent.

Her stomach growled, reminding her she hadn't eaten anything since yesterday. Having spent the day looking for a job, she hadn't gotten around to it. Now, she didn't know how long her money would have to last.

She turned the corner into an alley and began checking dumpsters along the narrow lane. The boutiques that fronted Franklin Street were ritzy, and she hoped they had tossed some slightly irregular articles, maybe even a coat, into the trash. She normally had more class than to go dumpster diving, but damn, she was cold tonight.

As she hurried across the street toward the next section of alley, the wind caught her, blowing dirt and leaves into her face.

"Shit." She stumbled into the alley out of the wind, wiping at her eyes.

"Give me your money." A rough voice came from the other side of a stack of boxes and Mert immediately froze. She heard scuffling and several grunts, then something heavy skidded to a stop against her boot. She looked down at the glint of a gun.

Cautiously she peeked around the crates to see a man, arms pinned behind his back by another, with a third man pounding him in the stomach. Knowing firsthand about violence, she quickly picked up the gun and pointed it at the men, thinking to use it only to get them to stop hitting.

"Leave him alone or I'll shoot," she yelled. Her hands shook so hard she knew if she had to, she'd probably shoot the innocent man instead of the thugs beating on him.

"Stay out of this, bitch!" One of the men yelled as he dug through the man's pockets.

Mert pointed the gun in the air, shut her eyes and squeezed the trigger. The blast echoed down the alley and slammed her on her butt, but it was enough to scare away the two men, who fled without looking back. Mert threw the gun aside and crawled over to where the man sat slumped against the brick wall.

* * *

Royal Bradford tried to focus on the face above him, but his vision kept blurring around the edges. He struggled upright only to fall back down. He swung an arm, hoping to deflect the thief.

"Yeah, right, like you're going to take me on," a feminine voice said as cold fingers clutched his wrist, helping him to his feet.

He staggered, leaning against the wall for support.

The girl moved to his side, sliding an arm around his waist. With her shoulder under his arm, she supported him the best she could for her size.

"Hey, watch where you put your paws." She swatted at his hand when he accidentally touched a soft, plump breast. "Where's your car?" she asked as she led him down the alley toward the street.

Royal had brought a cab downtown, and now he raised a hand to hail a hack, groaning at the tug of bruised muscles. He tried to straighten as the driver pulled to a stop in front of them, although he liked the feel of his rescue angel tucked close to his side.

He gritted his teeth as he reached for the door of the taxi. "Get in," he told the girl.

She seemed reluctant, so he groaned again and leaned more heavily against her. With a sigh, she helped him onto the seat, then scooted in beside him, slamming the door behind her.

He gave the driver his address then rested his head against the back of the seat. He couldn't summon the energy to speak, but wasn't about to let his rescuer out of his sight without properly thanking her.

* * *

"Good evening, Doctor," George said when he opened the door. "My word, what happened to you?"

"Minor skirmish," Royal answered the butler as the girl helped him into the house. He knew his lip was cut and his ribs bruised, but he felt much better than he had at first.

"You a doc?" the girl asked as she helped him out of his coat.

"Doctor of Philosophy." He stifled a groan. "We'll be in the study, George," he said. "Come along," he added to the girl. He didn't know what to do with her, but since she had practically saved his life, he felt he owed her something.

"You a shrink?"

His shoulders tightened. "That would be psychology or psychiatry."

"Yeah, so, if you ain't a head doctor, what are you?" She flopped into his favorite chair, swinging a leg over the arm.

He looked at her more closely. If not for her voice, he wouldn't at first have known she was female for she was dressed in combat boots, jeans and an oversized green army jacket. She pulled a knit cap off her head and a tumble of jet-black hair fell around her shoulders. Her face was pretty, even if she wore far too much makeup. And she was a woman, not a girl, though her petite frame had made him think she was quite young.

"Are you what they call Goth?"

She snorted. "Shit, no. Do I look Goth?"

"Well, I don't exactly know as I've never had the privilege of meeting one who is Goth."

"Is that what your kind of doctor does – talk funny?"

He poured himself a brandy. "A doctor of philosophy studies the way men think."

"That's a shrink."

"No, I look at the reasons behind the thinking, and what exactly they think about beliefs and values."

"Geez, that sounds boring as hell. You gonna offer me a drink?"

"Are you old enough?"

"Shit, doc, I've been drinking since I was fifteen."

He poured her a dainty portion of brandy, handing her the crystal snifter. She gulped it down and then gasped as the heat hit her.

He smiled, then grimaced when the cut on his lip stung. "And that would be exactly how many months go?"

"Cute, doc." She coughed.

"Please don't call me that. My name is Royal. Royal Bradford, to be precise. I guess we never formally introduced ourselves."

Instead of telling him her name in return, she stood, tossed the snifter at him and wandered around the room. He barely managed to catch the heirloom crystal to prevent it from shattering against the desk.

"Holy crap, you've got a pool," she exclaimed when she got to the double doors that opened onto the conservatory where Royal had recently added a lap pool.

"Yes—"

"Can I swim?" She turned her head to give him a smile and he immediately revised his thoughts of her being just pretty. Her smile dazzled him.

"You don't have a suit…" His voice trailed off as she opened the doors wide, stepped onto the tile and immediately began taking her clothes off.

Royal didn't stop her. Nor did he blink as her jacket dropped to the ground, followed by an oversized sweater. He gulped. She wasn't wearing a bra. When she bent over to unlace her boots, her jeans stretched tight over shapely buttocks and long legs.

He finally remembered to breathe when she dove into the heated water, swimming to the other end with long, sure strokes. His hands shook as he poured himself another drink.

She was coarse, rather rag-tag, and he didn't even know her name, but he wanted her in a primal way he had never felt before. Maybe the fact they appeared so opposite turned him on. He laughed at himself, thinking it was more likely the sight of her bare bottom and pale skin.

Royal watched her frolic in the pool like a water nymph. He had spent most of his life studying but not participating in life. He was fascinated by the critical examination of the rationale for man's most fundamental beliefs, but right at the moment, he began to wonder if he hadn't missed out on something more important.

He wasn't a virgin, heaven forbid, but sex had been used as part of his research. The mechanics, the physical elements, the sexual pheromones men and women exuded when mating – those clinical aspects were all part of one or the other research paper he had published over the years as they related to a particular culture's belief system. But the elemental surge of lust in his groin at this precise moment would be impossible to describe in a paper.

"Come in with me," she yelled from the edge of the pool, where she jumped up and down, giving him a tantalizing glimpse of breast.

In a daze, he sauntered over, squatting down at the edge. "Do you need to call someone? Don't you have to get home?"

Her smile disappeared. Before Royal could question her further, she pushed off and swam rapidly away from him. He could see her sleek, naked body beneath the rippling water and with a sigh, went in search of a robe.

* * *

Mert felt the sting of tears as she furiously cut through the water. Why did he have to be so nice? She was used to rude and offensive, or even being ignored on the jobs she had worked over the years. She didn't know how to react to nice. In a matter of minutes, he had broken through the tough shell she had wrapped around herself for the past seven years.

She turned at the other end and swam underwater, holding her breath until she felt her lungs would burst. She hated that the splendor of his home reminded her of what she had given up years ago. The warmth of the pool might make her hesitate to go back into the chilly October wind, but she told herself this was just make-believe and it didn't really exist for her.

Gasping for breath, she popped to the surface to find him standing at the edge of the pool, a large fluffy white robe in his hands and a soft smile on his lips.

"I don't even know your name, nor have I properly thanked you for saving my life." He held up the robe as she climbed the steps out of the water, but she noticed he didn't avert his gaze. Instead of finding his stare offensive as she often did when men ogled her, a warm feeling spread through her body.

She slipped her arms into the robe. When his hands touched her shoulders, she turned to face him. He glanced down, and without a word he pulled the robe together and tied the belt snuggly at her waist.

"We need to talk."

Talk, Mert could handle, she thought as she followed him back into the study. He had lit a fire and she moved closer to its warmth. A shiver went through her at the thought of not having a place to sleep tonight.

He handed her a cup of steaming coffee, then nodded towards the couch.

"Thanks," she said as she gladly accepted the drink. She gathered the extra-large robe around her as she sat, glad that the man sat across from her rather than on the couch beside her.

She studiously tried to ignore him as she sipped her coffee. She didn't know what he wanted, but she wasn't naive enough to think he was being nice just as a favor to her. In her estimation, men weren't nice for no reason.

"First, you must tell me your name so I can properly thank you."

His voice, soft and deep, stirred her from her reverie. She turned her gaze from the fire to study him. He had dwarfed her five foot four inch height when she had helped him from the alley. Now, as he casually reclined in a wing chair, legs outstretched, she was even more aware of his size. She remembered the strength of his arms and the feel of a tight stomach beneath his coat. His light brown hair was tousled, as though he continually ran his fingers through it. Clear blue eyes held her gaze, a strong square chin, straight nose and high cheekbones gave him the air of a man of the world. A very handsome man and Mert felt an odd sensation in the pit of her stomach.

"Mert."

"I beg your pardon?"

"My name," she said, not willing to give him any more information than necessary.

His brow furrowed. "What kind of name is that?"

"What kind of name is Royal?" she shot back.

"Touché." He smiled and Mert felt the funny little quivers again. "Well, Miss Mert, you have my eternal gratitude for stepping in as you did and saving me from disaster."

"Anyone with half a brain would know better than to be in that area of town late at night."

"You were there."

"Yeah, well, I'm from that area." She glanced at his neatly creased, although stained, slacks and obviously expensive sweater. She allowed her gaze to drift around the room, past luxurious furniture and plush area rugs. "You obviously ain't."

"And that brings us back to my original question."

Mert was going to make him ask; she wouldn't volunteer anything.

"Miss Mert?"

She gave an exaggerated sigh. "I ain't a prissy miss, okay? It's Meredith." She frowned at him just to let him know she wasn't happy telling him.

"That's not the question I was asking, but thank you for telling me." He took a sip of brandy. "Do you need to call anyone to let them know you're all right?"

She glanced again at the fine furnishings and gleaming hardwood floors. He was one of them – the rich, snooty people who thought they could get away with anything just because they had money. Suddenly she wanted to strike out at him; to shock his rich, snooty ears.

"I got locked out of my fucking apartment for not paying the rent. I lost my job last week so no way can I pay the fucking rent."

"I'm sorry," he said softly. If he was shocked, he didn't show it. "In that case, the least I can do is offer you a room for the night and breakfast in the morning. George makes quite an omelet."

* * *

Royal gave up trying to make sense of his notes. Tossing his pen on the desk, he ran his hands through his hair as he walked over to the

104

conservatory doors. After ensconcing Meredith in the yellow room upstairs, he had come back to the study and tried to concentrate on his latest work, even though his muscles screamed in protest. But all he could think about was her sleeping naked. He had no doubt that she was, for she didn't have anything with her, and her rumpled clothes still lay on the tile by the pool.

He smiled. Meredith no-last-name was a creature beyond his understanding. He had the feeling she had spent much of her life looking out for herself, and she was certainly streetwise. In his philosophical studies over the years, he thought he had seen just about everything. He always tried to look beneath the surface of a person, and beyond the actual words they spoke. For that reason, he realized she had tried to shock him with her language when he knew there was more to her than she was willing to show him. He suspected her tough exterior held a gentle heart, or she never would have stepped into the middle of his troubles in the alley.

His brow cleared as a plan began to form. Meredith needed help, whether she wanted to accept it or not. And she could help him gain that which had rapidly been slipping beyond his grasp.

* * *

The minute Royal saw Meredith peeking around the doorframe the next morning, he waved her in, cutting his aunt off in mid-tirade and hanging up the phone. Sometime last night, she had come back for her clothes and he frowned at her appearance. She should dress like a woman, he thought, and she would, if she accepted his plan.

"I have a proposition for you," he began.

"I don't turn tricks."

"Tricks? I...oh. No, that's not what I meant." His mouth lifted in humor but seeing her scowl, he quickly turned serious. "Would you marry me?"

Meredith fell into the chair next to his desk. "I don't even know you."

He waved a hand in dismissal. "It wouldn't be a real marriage. Just a..." How could he come up with the right words to gain her compliance? "Aha! A marriage of convenience."

She scowled again. "There's nothing convenient about marriage." She rose and moved toward the door. "Thanks for the bed."

Royal hurried around the corner of his desk, grabbing her arm to stop her. She tried to pull away, her previously passive mask turning to fear. He quickly released her, holding his hands in the air to show her he meant no harm.

"Give me five minutes to explain. Please."

She seemed to contemplate that for a moment.

"It ain't like I've got any place to be." She moved back to the chair, slinging one leg over the arm of it, swinging her foot.

He cringed at her language, starting to rethink his plan. She was pretty enough, and he knew for a fact she had a great figure, but if he was to make his aunt believe it was a love match, well, he had his work cut out for him.

He began to pace, if only so he couldn't stare at the sight of her, slouched in his chair, her femininity spread wide. He envisioned her as she had been last night in the pool, the black curls at her feminine core glistening with water droplets. He wondered if she would be just as wet...

"Four minutes."

He cleared his throat. "My father came from an old established family here in Philadelphia and because he had only one sister, he naturally ran the family businesses and inherited the majority of the wealth. This house," he spread his arms to encompass his home, "dates back to the revolutionary war and has been the home to generations of Bradfords."

"Doc, I'm glad you got a pedigree, but that don't exactly seem a reason to get married."

"Heritage and family lines meant everything to my father, who passed away last year. According to his will, if I don't marry before I turn thirty-two, everything goes to my aunt's son, who already has a gaggle of children."

"How long you got?"

"I'll turn thirty-two in just two weeks."

"So why ain't you married?" she asked, then added, "You're gay." It wasn't a question.

He frowned. "I am not. I've simply spent my life studying philosophy, not chasing women, and while my father was alive I never really thought about marrying."

"And now you have to, just to keep all your money."

He ran a hand through his hair. "It's not the money at all."

"Yeah, right. It's always about the fucking money. Otherwise my shit of a landlord wouldn't have locked me out of my apartment."

Royal realized that all the ethical and moral reasons in the world wouldn't win her compliance, but money, regardless of what she said, could.

"I'll give you fifty thousand dollars if you agree to be my wife before my birthday to satisfy the terms of my father's will."

"What?" she squawked, coming up out of the chair. "Fifty thousand bucks to pretend?"

Royal shook his head. "Not pretend. I'm sure my aunt will demand a legitimate marriage certificate."

"So it's fifty thou to fuck me?"

"No!" Royal shouted, frustrated that she didn't understand, or maybe he just wasn't explaining it right. "I mean, we will be married, but I wouldn't presume to impose myself on you." Even as he said it, he found himself wondering what it would be like to sink into her hot body; to caress and suckle at her breasts.

"Your time's up, Doc." Meredith walked toward the door.

Royal was beside himself. "Okay, one hundred thousand."

She turned at that, her green eyes shooting sparks. "Fuck you, your money and your damned heritage. Marriage means fists and drunken arguments. And all the money in the world ain't going to make me buy into that."

Royal realized that someone in her past had hurt her, which was probably the reason she had reacted so badly when he had grabbed her arm. He knew he needed to change tactics, quickly. He moved in front of the door, blocking her exit but not touching her.

"It's snowing." He said the first thing that came to mind; anything to get her to stop for a minute so he could regroup.

She turned to look out the window and then groaned.

"Look, you don't have a place to stay and the weather is not conducive to sleeping in the park. I want to continue living in my home and conducting my research. We can help each other."

"I don't want your money." She straightened her spine and stuck her chin out at a stubborn angle and Royal had the feeling she hadn't always been from the wrong side of town. There was breeding in her stance.

"Fine. We'll get married," at her look he hurried on, "but only pretend to have a marriage. You will have your own room, clothes, food, anything you want." He watched her relax just slightly. "And in return, you will pretend to be my devoted wife. But you'll have to dress decently and quit using foul language."

"*Fuck* you," she said.

Regardless of what he said about her language, the way she said fuck made him want to take her right there on the floor. Now, he didn't think; he just acted, circling her waist and pulling her close as his mouth came down on hers. She tasted of coffee and woman, exotic and forbidden, and he drank his fill.

Somewhere in the endless time they stood there, Royal realized she was kissing him back, her tongue plunging into his mouth, her hips sliding sensuously against his.

"Okay, fine, I'll do it," she gasped when they broke apart, "but only for a place to stay. And you gotta quit kissing me like that."

He looked at her glittering green eyes and rosy, kiss-swollen lips and wondered what he had gotten himself into. As she moved away, his body made him painfully aware that a marriage of convenience was not going to be as easy as he first thought.

* * *

What had she gotten herself into? Mert twisted the plain gold ring on her finger. Within

110

a day, Royal had gotten a license and they had been married by a judge at the courthouse. Then he had spent days correcting her language and etiquette and shopping for clothes, most of which were still piled on her bed.

She had a flashback to her past. Her stepfather, who drank too much and abused her mother, had always bought her expensive things by way of apology. After her mother had died, he had turned his tirades on her until, at sixteen, she had run away. She had lived on the streets until she found a job and she'd shared a variety of crummy apartments with a number of equally crummy roommates. Regardless of how hard up she ever got, she had sworn she'd never go back or ask him for help.

And now, look what she had done. Was this any different, allowing Royal to buy her things and living in wealth? Had she sold herself after all? She sighed. She was just so tired of living hand to mouth.

Besides, she had laid alone in her bed on her wedding night, and somewhere deep in her heart she knew Royal was different. He hadn't even kissed her good night, reminding her they were just pretending to be married.

Damn it, she didn't want to pretend. At least, she didn't think she did. Royal's gentle spirit tugged at her heart and she longed to wipe away the serious expression he usually wore. Besides, she was hot for his body.

She checked herself in the mirror and pulled off the top that covered her swimsuit.

From the one kiss they had shared, she knew
Royal wanted her. He had been hot and hard as
he pressed against her, and he made her ache in
all the right places. She had told him not to kiss
her again, but if she gave herself freely to him, it
wouldn't be changing their bargain, and she
could still leave when the charade was over. She
rubbed a hand over a soft cashmere sweater.
How hard was it going to be to leave all this
behind for the second time in her life?

With a sigh, she wandered from the room,
her bath towel trailing behind her. As she hoped,
Royal was in his study.

"Want to go for a swim with me?" she
asked as she entered.

"No, go ahead," he replied without looking
up.

Mert was disappointed until she heard him
cough and sputter as she opened the doors to the
pool area. She smiled a secret smile, determined
to make Royal more interested in physiology
than philosophy.

* * *

Royal was waiting for her at the edge of the
pool, a hard-on straining the fabric of his slacks
so badly he could hardly walk. Meredith had
been taunting him with her luscious body from
the first day they met, and the scrap of fabric

she called a swimming suit left little to the imagination.

He had promised not to impose on her, but damn, he wanted her. Regardless of her language, which had cleaned up remarkably well and quite quickly, he knew innately she came from good breeding, and perhaps that was why he hesitated. He thought it might have been easier to take her to his bed if she had continued to curse, because what he wanted to do with her had no gentle names, and he had never felt so out of control in his life.

He wanted to fuck her – hard, fast and more than once. He ached to taste her and have her return the favor. He wondered what the new, lady-like Meredith would say to that.

"I just got off the phone with my aunt," he said the minute she stopped at the wall, knowing he had to get his mind out of the gutter. "She's insisting on throwing us a wedding reception at the Ritz-Carlton in two weeks. I'm sure it's her way of putting us in the spotlight, hoping to publicly defraud me." He watched her frown. "Do you think you'll be ready?"

Royal had insisted she practice being a lady in everything she did, from eating to speaking to how she sat and walked. It hadn't been hard for Mert to remember her manners, or even how to speak properly since the first sixteen years of her life had meant nannies and private schools and then the country club set. But she refused to divulge that to Royal. Let him think she was a quick study, or that he was a brilliant teacher.

"So that means more lessons today?" she asked as she popped out of the pool. She shook her head, deliberately splattering him with water. He didn't get mad; in fact he stood as though rooted to the spot and she could have sworn she saw steam rise. While he stared at her chest, she glanced down to see his trousers were tented. She took a step closer.

Her movement seemed to break his trance. He quickly backed up and cleared his voice.

"Get some clothes on then we'll talk." He walked away but Mert could have sworn she heard him groan, and that was before he walked right into a chaise lounge.

* * *

Mert was back down in the study half an hour later, but when Royal began a discussion on philosophy, she wrinkled her nose in disgust.

"Can't we discuss the Phillies game or something?" she asked.

He looked at the papers on his desk. "Why? Demetrios Andreas was one of the leading philosophers of the last century and his works are still studied today. In fact, he--"

"He's dead," she interrupted. "Who cares what he thought?"

"His writings are central in the intellectual history of men."

"You always say men. Don't you believe women think?"

"I use men in the generic sense."

"You use men?" she repeated, then grinned. "I knew you were gay."

His mouth dropped open before he sputtered, "You can't keep saying whatever pops into your head, Meredith. I thought we were making progress."

With perfect elocution and a straight face, she said, "Do excuse my slip of the tongue. Whatever was I thinking?" She sashayed up to him, her hands clasped with ladylike decorum.

He burst out laughing, grabbing her in a hug. "I don't ever remember laughing this much before you came into my life."

She joined his mirth, returning his hug and suddenly the air felt charged with electricity. Royal's body sprang to life and he pulled her hips snug, wanting her to know how much she turned him on.

"Doc?" She said the word with hesitancy, curiosity, hunger; and he answered the only way he could.

She groaned in surrender when his lips crushed hers, her arms tightening around him and her hips nudging his groin.

"I want you desperately," he moaned into her mouth, his hands sliding up her ribs to cup her breasts.

"I won't sell my body for a roof over my head." She said the words even as she caressed him, making him strain against his pants.

Royal couldn't think. She was driving him to the brink of insanity, but somewhere in the corner of his mind, he understood her concerns.

"No, it wouldn't be like that."

Her mouth was back on his. She circled his neck; he cupped her buttocks and lifted so she could lock her legs behind his back.

"Bedroom." He muttered as he hurried down the hall and up the stairs. He could feel her heat and couldn't wait to get her naked.

Kicking his bedroom door shut behind them, he dropped her onto the bed, then yanked down her slacks, followed by bikini underwear as she jerked off her sweater. He kissed her belly button, her hips, then trailed his tongue across her skin to her breasts. She stretched beneath him, spreading her legs and rubbing her mound against his stomach. The minute he sucked her nipple into his mouth, she arched.

"I've got to touch you," she moaned, yanking his shirt out of his pants.

Royal reluctantly released her breast so he could undress. As he kicked off his shoes and fumbled with his slacks, Meredith came up on her elbows, openly watching his every move. Her feet were flat on the bed, her knees spread wide, and he couldn't get his clothes off fast enough.

When he shrugged out of his briefs and reached for her, she scrambled to her knees.

"Wait." She held him in place with her palms on his chest, caressing his muscles, then tweaking his nipples. She put hot lips to his breastbone, then began a slow, torturous descent, her kisses getting longer and harder as she lowered her head.

Royal's knees buckled, and if not for the edge of the bed, he would have fallen down.

"Stop! I've got to have you right this minute." He lifted her head and she gazed up at him, her glistening lips lifting in a seductive smile.

"But what about the marriage just for convenience?"

He flipped her back onto the bed, coming down on her and sliding to heaven with one long stoke.

"It won't change anything, I swear."

But it changed everything.

* * *

For the next two days, lessons were forgotten. Unless, Royal thought, the many positions they tried during their love making marathons could be considered part of his or Meredith's education. She was vigorous and wild in bed, but she continued to remind him that having sex with him was of her own free will and had nothing to do with the room, board and clothes he provided. And he continued to agree with her if only to make her happy.

He had always been quite reserved and in control, but with Meredith, he felt free. He had been expressing that freedom by taking her in just about every room of the house and as he slid in and out of her hot, slick depths, he would shout out in climax.

Now, he dropped his head against the shower wall, letting the water beat over him. Meredith had done more than take up lodging in one of the many bedrooms of his house. She had invaded him; mind, body and soul and he was beginning to wonder why they had to dissolve their marriage after his birthday. He knew for a fact his feelings ran deeper than the gratitude he had first felt.

"Can I join you?" Meredith peeked around the edge of the shower stall.

He didn't bother correcting her grammar but smiled and grabbed her hand, pulling her under the water with him. "You're like Jell-O. I always have room for you."

Meredith groaned. "Oh my God, the doc made a joke. A bad one, but still a joke."

"And you make me happy," Royal murmured as he took her mouth in a searing kiss. As always, their passion skyrocketed. He kissed her neck, her shoulder, bending down to take a nipple into his mouth. She had her hand on him, stroking, making him swell.

"Sit," he moaned, easing her back onto the tiled ledge at one end of the shower. He knelt in front of her, brushing her wet hair back from her face, tracing the arch of her brow with his finger. God, he had fallen hard for this woman.

"Meredith, I—"

She put a finger to his lips. "Just do it, doc."

118

Royal wasn't about to deny either of them that pleasure. As she caressed his back and shoulders, he nuzzled her breasts, licking and sucking first one then the other. The water beat against his back as he showered her with affection. Sliding his hands down her thighs, he pushed her knees apart, kissing a hot trail down her stomach. He nipped her hip with his teeth then soothed her with kisses. No matter how many times they made love, each was a new experience. She grabbed his hair as he teased her and he could feel her muscles clutch around his invading fingers.

"More," she whispered raggedly and he complied until she fell apart, her legs trembling as the sensations shot out in all directions.

He lifted her and turned so he could sit on the ledge with her straddling his lap. This time she reached down between them to caress him before lifting her hips and sliding down all the way, burying him deep.

He gazed into her glittering green eyes. "How many do you want, sweetheart?"

She wrapped her arms around his neck as she moved up, and then slowly back down, squeezing her muscles around him. She gave him a siren's smile. "I'll have to settle for three. We're running out of hot water."

* * *

It was the day of their reception, and Mert hoped she passed inspection. She thought about her combat boots and army jacket, hidden in the bottom of the closet, and knew she would be more comfortable in those than the fancy dress and heels she was to wear. She had been born to wealth and privilege, even if she hadn't been living like it for the past seven years. Regardless, her stomach churned in nervous distress.

For Royal's sake, she hoped she didn't forget herself and screw up. She was beginning to care for him, nerd that he was. He was always so serious about his philosophy, but he loosened up fast when they had sex. With him, she forgot her past and lived only for the pleasure he gave her. A pleasure she needed now.

"Hey, Doc," she said, rolling to the side where he laid naked on her bed. She caressed his bare chest.

"Hey, Mert," he mimicked, using her nickname even though she knew he preferred to call her Meredith.

"When we're not around your aunt or anybody, can I say what I want?"

He frowned at her; the hand that had idly been caressing her hip paused. "You're always free to say what you want to me. You should know that by now."

She leaned forward, licking his nipple and watching it pebble. She smiled. Her hand slid down his chest to his groin.

"Okay, then would you fuck me?"

Laughing, he rolled over, pushing her to her back and settling between her legs. She raised her knees, planting her feet on the bed and pushing up against him. The ache in her grew.

"Would you fuck me, please?" he corrected.

* * *

Mert's fingers dug into Royal's arm. "Who are all these people?" she whispered, panicking at the sight of a huge crowd only two steps below her in the ballroom of the Ritz.

Royal shrugged easily. "Mostly business associates."

"You're a nerdy scholar," she replied. "What kind of business?"

He smiled, the sexy smile that always made Mert's stomach flip. He bent to kiss her cheek.

"Thanks for putting me in my place, as usual."

"Seriously, Royal…"

"I don't physically manage any of the businesses that are part of Bradford Enterprises, but I am the majority stockholder and Chairman of the Board."

"Fu—" Mert caught herself just in time.

She felt Royal tense. "Look out, here comes my aunt," he said in a low tone.

"Oh, lord," Mert moaned.

He covered her hand with his. "You'll do fine."

"Royal, how nice to finally meet your bride," the bleach blonde, perfectly made up woman practically purred. Mert hated her on sight.

"Aunt Saundra, I'm delighted to introduce my wife, Meredith Bradford."

"How did you two meet?" His aunt started right in with the questions, deliberately ignoring Mert's outstretched hand.

"It was a small gathering," Royal replied, giving Mert a wink. "My first glimpse of Meredith and I fell at her feet."

Mert laughed, his satirical humor putting her at ease. Royal was playing his aunt and she didn't even realize it.

"Well, shall we get things moving?" Saundra said in a sickly sweet voice. The look she gave Mert as she raised a hand to the orchestra made her realize the woman thought she would fall on her face the minute she moved.

She slid a hand down the slinky, midnight blue dress she wore and took a deep breath. She only hoped she didn't prove the woman right.

"Ladies and gentlemen," a disembodied voice came over the loud speaker. "Presenting Mr. and Mrs. Royal Anthony Bradford." The orchestra began and Royal guided her down the steps and onto the dance floor.

His hand was warm on her bare back as he pulled her close and they began to dance.

"You mocked your aunt," she scolded him.

He shrugged. "She needed it. Don't think she won't cut you down if given the chance."

Mert put her head on his shoulder and they danced in companionable silence. She could stay like this forever, she thought, enjoying the security of his arms and the happiness in her heart.

Too soon, applause erupted as the dance ended and well-wishers surrounded them. Mert nodded politely at the many introductions, knowing she'd never remember any names.

In minutes, several people separated her and Royal, all pushing close until Mert thought she couldn't breathe.

"What the hell are you trying to pull?" A rough voice ground out as a hand grabbed her upper arm and squeezed painfully before jerking her around.

Mert looked into the bloodshot eyes of her stepfather.

"Let go." She tried to step away, her stomach twisting agonizingly.

John Butler took another gulp of drink. "If I'd known you'd sell yourself to the highest bidder, I would have bought you years ago."

Mert sucked in a breath at his insinuation.

"Butler," Royal's voice came from behind her. "I see you've met—" His eyes blazed with fury when he saw John's hand clamped around her arm. "What the hell? Get your hands off my wife."

"Royal." Mert put a hand to his chest to calm him. A scene like this was just what his aunt wanted. Luckily, her stepfather released her, but it didn't dim the murderous look Royal gave him.

"Get the hell out of here," Royal hissed at John before taking her hand to lead her in the opposite direction. She stumbled in her high heels trying to keep up with him.

"Royal, slow down. People are staring."

Her words finally penetrated and he paused, circling her shoulders as he said softly, "Sorry." He didn't speak again until they were out of the ballroom and in a small alcove.

"How do you know John Butler?"

Mert's stomach sank. She really didn't want to have this discussion. She knew now she loved Royal, and he would hate her when he found out.

"Meredith?"

"How do you?" she asked instead of answering.

"He's president of one of the Bradford Enterprises' companies."

Oh God, this was worse than she imagined. Tears welled in her eyes and she was suddenly enveloped in warmth as Royal pulled her against his chest and wrapped his arms around her.

"Sweetheart tell me."

"He's my step-father," she whispered, her shoulders tensing as she waited for his rejection.

Instead of pushing her away, he pulled her closer.

"I don't understand. Your last name was Olson."

She sniffled. "He married my mother when I was four, but he never adopted me."

"Then why were you in such dire straits? Why hasn't he taken care of you?" The anger was back in his voice.

She buried her face against his chest, not wanting to see his reaction when she disclosed her secret.

"He abused my mother. When she died, he turned his attentions on me."

"He raped you?"

"No, just punched on me when he got drunk, which was often. Until I finally ran away."

He held her from him and when she wouldn't look at him, he lifted her chin, forcing her to meet his gaze.

"Meredith, this isn't your fault."

"I didn't stop him!" she cried.

"Honey, you were a child." He wrapped her in his arms again, rocking her gently. "That bastard will never work in this town again."

"I'm sorry, Royal. If your aunt finds out, she'll no doubt find a way to have our marriage annulled. I'm not exactly good heritage wife material."

"Nonsense. You're brave and resilient and you have more courage than I would ever have. I love you just the way you are."

"You—" Mert never got a chance to finish as his lips closed over hers in a kiss that was both tender and seductive.

"Let's go home."

As they stepped back into the ballroom, Mert had yet another shock as she caught sight of a man talking to Aunt Saundra.

She tugged Royal to a stop. "Who's that man speaking to your aunt?"

Royal scanned the crowd. "That's Saundra's son, Paul. Why?"

Mert knew him in a different venue but before she could say anything, Saundra came bearing down on them.

"Royal, I just spoke with John Butler. Your wife has been living on the streets, for God's sake." She clutched a hand to her throat. "We'll have something to say to the lawyers about this."

Mert thought she sounded more delighted than troubled.

Royal started to speak but Mert put a hand on his arm. He had said he loved her, and she wouldn't let him lose his heritage to this woman.

"Darling," she spoke softly. "Would you get me some champagne while I visit with your aunt?" When he gave her a questioning look, she smiled and added, "Please?"

His eyes lit at her reminder of their earlier grammar lesson.

The minute he was out of hearing, she turned to Saundra, her eyes narrowed and her voice low and menacing. "You will not threaten Royal. You see, I know your son and if you even think about doing anything that will hurt Royal or his life, I will turn Pauly in for drug trafficking."

The older woman gasped. "That's a lie."

Mert slowly shook her head. "I know people. I finger them and they finger your son."

"That's blackmail!"

Mert smiled. "Yeah, well, that's what happens, whether you come from a gated community or from the streets. You meet all kinds of filth and you learn the worst about most of them."

By the time Royal returned, his aunt was nowhere to be seen. He handed her a flute of champagne and saluted her with his glass. Mert let the rest of her past slide from her shoulders as she looked at her lover, her husband, and knew she had given away her heart.

* * *

Mert wandered around Royal's study while he attended to all the paperwork at the lawyers. It was his birthday and Mert wished she could think of something special to give him. After all, he had nailed her stepfather and given her back her life. How could she ever repay that?

She glanced at the clutter of papers on his desk and absently began gathering them up.

Over the past few weeks, she had become just slightly fond of that Andreas guy, as long as Royal explained what he was saying in words she could understand. She picked up a paper written in Royal's dark scribble; notes he had made, no doubt. She started to put it on the stack when the words caught her eyes.

Demetrios Andreas writes mostly on man's preoccupation with material things and that man's existence depends on the romance of wealth, or perhaps the tragedy of it. For man seems disinclined to be satisfied with what he has, and is in eternal pursuit of that which he has not.

There are no other records of Andreas' writings, though they have been sought after to no avail for many years. From my research on Andreas, I have concluded that any man's wealth comes not from what he possesses, but what he gives. For only in giving will he gain a hundred fold – no, a hundred thousand times, that which he has given.

The paper drifted from Mert's grasp as she realized she had the perfect gift for Royal.

* * *

It was dark as Royal pulled up to his house. The wind circled the drive and he looked up, wondering if it would snow tonight.

128

"Good evening, Doctor." George met him at the door as he always did. "Miss Meredith requests your presence in the conservatory."

"Thank you, George." Royal wandered into his study, dropping his briefcase on a chair as he glanced toward the double doors of the conservatory. It was pitch black in there. Perhaps Meredith wasn't...

He heard a splash and smiled, thinking his entire house could burn down around their ears and she would be happy if only the pool were left.

"Meredith?" he called her as he opened the doors. When she didn't reply, he flipped the switch to the pool lights.

A ripple spread across the water, glittering in the low glow of the light. As he stood transfixed, Meredith rose from the water and slowly climbed the steps from the pool. Her body shimmered as silvery drops of water ran down her pale, naked skin. She reached up and slicked back her hair, the movement causing her breasts to lift, the nipples peaking. She walked toward him and Royal's whole body shook.

"Make love to me," she whispered, her voice sultry.

Royal realized that he had finally found his own philosophy of life in a black haired, smiling water nymph. He scooped her up and carried her upstairs as fast as he could to put that philosophy into practice.

* * *

They lay in bed, naked and sweating from making love, but Mert was ready to cry. Royal had his heritage and she knew it was time to leave. Though she had given herself freely to him and he had made love to her as achingly sweet as always, they had an agreement and about the only thing she had left to her name was her honor. She would never love another like she did him.

"I heard some interesting news today," he said as he rolled to his side facing her. He absently swirled a finger around her breasts and down her stomach. "It seems the police received a tip that my cousin has been dealing drugs."

"Oh." Mert's heart beat faster. Saundra had tried to cause trouble for Royal and Mert had made good on her promise.

His lips tilted in a slight smile. "Yes. It seems that someone pointed a finger at someone else and … well, you probably know how that story goes." He kissed her chin. "Thank you," he whispered softly. "You didn't need to put yourself in danger for me."

"I was afraid your aunt would contest everything." Mert bit her lip. "After we go our separate ways, of course. Are you terribly mad that you retained your heritage but your name was besmirched?"

He laughed. "Hell, no. Scum like that needs to be behind bars so our children can grow up safe."

She sucked in a breath. Was it possible?

Royal reached beneath his pillow and pulled out a small box, opening it to reveal the largest diamond Mert had ever seen. "Will you marry me, Meredith, for real?"

"I'm already married," she blurted the first thing that came to mind. At his look of surprise, she added, just to make sure there were no misunderstandings. "A convenient sort of marriage, to a rather nerdy philosopher."

"Fuck him," Royal said with a frown although his eyes glittered.

She laughed out loud, pushing him to his back and straddling him. She kept her hands on his chest as she wiggled her butt.

"He's very proper, most of the time. I'm not sure he would like that."

Royal lifted her hips and slid into her and she groaned at the fullness. "Oh, he would like it, all right. In fact, I'll bet he'd like it right now."

Run For Your Life

Emily Patterson had escaped Chicago in the middle of the night with no more than the clothes on her back, even though she didn't think Douglas would really kill her. After all, they had lived together for two years. Surely that counted for something.

Shivering, she huddled deeper into her fur coat. She couldn't remember the last time she had slept. She should have known better than to drive through Colorado in winter, but then again, she hadn't been thinking clearly. If only she'd thought to change into something warmer; if only her car hadn't slid around that last curve and landed in the ditch. She sighed around another shiver, realizing her biggest regret—if only she hadn't tried to turn Douglas into the authorities.

Emily turned the ignition key, knowing she had to have heat as she tried to outlast the blizzard. She only ran the car for short times to heat the interior enough to keep from freezing. She had tried to call AAA on her cell phone, but there was no signal here in the mountains. Only afterward did she realize that Douglas might be able to trace the call. After all, he had bugged the apartment and the office.

She tried the ignition again. Nothing. She let out a cry of dismay when she looked at the fuel gauge. Why hadn't she paid more attention?

Emily started crying. She didn't want to die out here, all alone and cold. She was only twenty-six and had her whole life ahead of her. Or so she had thought until she discovered the financial firm where she worked was a front for money laundering, and Douglas Lattimer, her boyfriend who had gotten her the job, worked for the mob.

"Damn you!" she screamed into the night. "I will not let you do this to me!" She bundled her coat around her and jerked open the door. The blizzard had stopped, but the snow was still deep. As she trudged through drifts toward a light in the distance, she tried to keep her anger wrapped around her, warming her from the inside.

Soon, it did no good. Exhausted and cold to her very soul, she sank to the ground by a tree. She couldn't keep her eyes open; couldn't focus on moving. She'd just rest a minute, then go on. Her last conscious thought was a wish to wake up somewhere warm and wonderful where the mob couldn't touch her.

* * *

Even with winter in full force, Tyler Sheridan had been keeping the men at High Ridge Lumber Company busy in the sawmill and furniture barn. When spring arrived, they'd be ahead of the game with lumber ready for construction and of course, there were always handcrafted furniture orders. Tonight, however, everything had come to a standstill. The men were in the bunkhouse waiting out the storm, which could last for days.

Tyler looked out the front window as an unusual array of lightning flashed and thunder blew in on the howling wind. Something was wrong. He could feel it in his bones; the uneasiness making his stomach roll and his head hurt. He bent to bank the fire in the huge fireplace, only to turn back when Blackie began growling at the front door of the cabin. Figuring he wouldn't get any rest until he investigated, he pulled on his heaviest coat, tugged a cap low over his ears, and walked out into the night. Even though the snow had stopped, he grabbed hold of the rope they had tied between the company office, the bunkhouse and the sawmill just to make sure he didn't wander too far off course in the inky blackness. As he carefully made his way across the compound, Blackie bounded ahead of him, undeterred by the drifts and cold.

The flashlight's beam was too small for Tyler to see the lump next to the tree until he practically tripped over it. He kept one hand clenched to the lifeline but in an effort to maintain his balance, dropped the flashlight and was immediately thrown into darkness. Feeling his way, he discovered the fur bundled shape was a person.

Knowing how fast the winter winds could kill, he didn't pause to investigate but picked up the surprisingly light figure and slung it over his shoulder. Holding it in place with one arm, he used his other hand to slide along the lifeline that would lead him back to the office. Stumbling as he kicked off his snowshoes on the porch, he heard a soft moan and knew a quick sense of relief that whoever it was, he was still alive.

"Get back." He pushed Blackie away when the dog stuck her nose close as Tyler laid his bundle on the fur rug as close to the fire as he dared. He tugged the fur hat off and long auburn hair spilled across his hand.

"Christ," he exclaimed, dropping back on his haunches as he turned her head toward him. Porcelain skin, a small, turned up nose and luscious pink lips created the picture of an angel; a very cold, unconscious one. He tore at the damp coat she wore, knowing he had to get her warm if she was to have any chance of surviving.

He undressed her as gently as he could, his body reacting to her loveliness with each piece of clothing he removed. His fingers lingered on the cleft between her breasts as he unhooked her bra; his eyes caressed her flat stomach and long, slender legs.

Another moan brought him out of his stupor. He grabbed the quilt from the sofa and wrapped it around her. She began thrashing from side to side and mumbling incoherently.

Tyler reached for her shoulders as she started to rise because he knew it was an unconscious movement. Her skin was icy, and his brain ran through the survival guide he had read not so long ago.

"Help me, dear God, help me," she cried as she flung her arms around him, burying her cold nose against his neck. Tyler knew only one way he could keep her still and get her warm at the same time. As she continued to cling to him, he struggled out of his own clothes.

* * *

Emily felt blessed heat surround her on all sides. Her face and hands tingled, but when she touched herself, she knew she was warm. As her hands traveled down her throat and across her shoulders, she also realized she was naked. Still, she couldn't rouse herself enough to worry because the warmth felt so good. She wiggled deeper beneath the soft quilt that was tucked under her chin and heard a groan from behind her. It wasn't until then that she realized the warmth behind her was coming from a body—a hard, very large, male body.

Dear God, Douglas had found her after all. She swiftly turned, ready to fight him and once again, run for her life. But the arm that circled her waist refused to release her and she found herself pulled against a warm, smooth chest. Her eyes flew open.

Brilliant blue eyes met hers; a generous mouth tilted into a grin.

"Hello," the mouth said, but Emily could only wonder how that mouth might feel on hers. The thought startled her. The man was a stranger, not Douglas at all, but then she should have guessed that with her eyes closed. Douglas was much smaller than this man; much leaner and not as strong. And she could see this man had dark hair and piercing eyes, whereas Douglas was fair-haired with light brown eyes.

"Where; how?" Questions flew through Emily's mind, but were rapidly being pushed aside by the heat from this man and the instant sexual attraction she felt. His eyes and his gentle hold told her without words she was safe. The hard evidence of his arousal probing her bare stomach indicated he felt the attraction as much as she did.

How was it possible to feel such fascination for a stranger? She could only think it was because of the trauma she had suffered. Her body certainly wanted to explore the attraction even as her brain urged caution. Her knee bent, allowing her leg to slide up the outside of his.

"My name's Emily," she whispered softly, her lips not touching him but oh, she wanted to.

"Tyler," he replied, the sound rumbling from deep in his chest, sending out vibes that caused her to shiver. "Are you cold?" His hand rubbed her back, inadvertently pulling her closer. "Do you need more warmth?"

"Yes," she told him, this time allowing her lips to barely brush the soft skin of his neck. He smelled like the outdoors.

He started to rise; perhaps to put more wood on the fire she could hear crackling behind her. She clutched his arms, holding him in place. His gaze came to rest on hers, the blue of his eyes turned dark with passion.

"Warm me," Emily begged, wanting something from this man, this stranger, that she couldn't define.

* * *

Tyler might have been as frozen as the snow banks for all that her words stopped him in motion. But as his gaze slid over her where the quilt had fallen away, his body temperature soared. With a groan, he dropped back to her side, scooping her up in his arms and rolling onto his back with her on top. His hand cupped the back of her neck and with little effort, he lowered her head until her lips touched his. Cool and smooth, they opened beneath his questing

138

tongue and within seconds, he was breathing the same air; tasting her sweetness, and those once chilly lips warmed under his caress.

When he slid his hands over her smooth bottom, she moaned softly, then dipped her knee between his legs and rubbed against him. He was hot and hard against her hip and he felt an acute desire to be deep inside her. Only when she ran a cold hand down his chest did he finally realize that he couldn't take her. Not that he wouldn't, if she stayed here for very long, but that he couldn't do it right now.

He broke the kiss and with gentle pressure tugged her head back to look into eyes the color of the forest in springtime.

"Emily?"

"Hmm?" Her head dropped to his chest and her hand relaxed. He waited another minute, barely breathing, wanting her so bad he ached. When she didn't move or utter another sound, he gently rolled her over onto the rug. Her eyes were closed, her breathing shallow. She was still cold to the touch, so he tugged the blanket up over both of them and settled in for the night.

He had no idea how this woman came to be at High Ridge, or how she had managed to survive in the bitter cold wind he could hear still howling outside. The reasons were irrelevant. She had ended up in his cabin and in his arms, and he intended to see that she stayed there.

* * *

Tyler wiped a sweaty arm across his brow. It shouldn't be so friggin' hot in the middle of December, he thought, rolling over.

"Stop!" A screech broke through his musings and he abruptly jerked awake. At the same time his fuzzy brain comprehended he held a squirming bundle in his arms, he felt the sting of a slap. His reflex action was to push, only to hear a thud and a soft, feminine "ouch."

"Oh, Christ, I'm sorry." He quickly knelt and rolled Emily back over. Her arm flopped to the side as she lay deadly still. He didn't have to touch her again to realize she was burning up with fever.

He lifted her in his arms and walked through the cabin to his bedroom and then into the bathroom. Trying to hold her steady on his lap while he started the water, he couldn't help but admire her naked beauty.

The minute he put her in the tepid water, she began thrashing, clawing at his bare arms with her red fingernails.

"Crap." He grabbed both hands and lifted them over her head only to have her start kicking as she jerked against his hold. Water went everywhere.

"Get away from me!" she hollered.

"Sh, baby. I'm trying to help." He kept his voice low, hoping to break through her delirium.

She whimpered and went limp. "Don't kill me, Douglas. You said you loved me; how can you kill me?" Her head rolled from side to side as she continued to mumble.

Tyler grabbed a rag and began sponging cool water across her hot skin. Over and over, he dribbled water across her chest and down her stomach, wringing the cloth and wiping her brow and face. He couldn't begin to understand who would want to harm such a beautiful woman or why.

Once she calmed and quit muttering, he continued to soothe her. When the cloth fell away, he used his hand, caressing her breasts, cupping water over her hips and legs, letting his fingers linger ever so briefly when her nipples pebbled under his touch.

With a sigh, he lifted her from the tub and carried her wet into the bedroom where he laid her on his bed. He figured her damp skin would continue to cool her, but he pulled a sheet up lightly over her anyway. She seemed to be resting, and he knew he would have to wait for answers to the hundred or so questions he had. As he glanced down at his unruly body, he figured he would have to wait for more than answers.

* * *

Emily rolled over and stretched. She loved Sundays. She could sleep late and Douglas would usually make her breakfast in bed, after he had waken her by...

Douglas!

She sat straight up, glancing wildly around but recognizing nothing. The rough plank walls, heavy wooden furniture and plaid spread on the bed didn't belong in her apartment in Chicago. Then she remembered—the wild flight from town, the days and nights without sleep until she was exhausted. But the last thing she remembered was the car sliding sideways into a ditch, so how did she end up here?

She could hear noise in the other room and decided it couldn't be Douglas if she was still alive. That didn't mean whoever was rattling around out there was a friend.

She stiffened her spine and her resolve as she swung her feet over the side of the bed and stood up. She had made up her mind and there was no turning back but she knew she had to proceed with caution. Not finding her clothes, she jerked the sheet off the bed and wrapped it around herself. As quietly as she could, she eased her way over to the open door and peeked around the doorframe.

She bit her tongue to keep the gasp from escaping. The most gorgeous man she had ever seen sat at a desk off to the side, his dark head bent over an open book. She could tell he was tall, even seated, and his shoulders were broad under the flannel shirt he wore. Corded muscles bunched and relaxed in his forearms as he wrote. His profile was strong, dark whiskers shadowing his chin and cheeks. She smiled when she saw him stick his tongue out to the side in concentration.

She knew him, yet couldn't place him. Jumbled thoughts rattled around in her brain of hot kisses and gentle hands, yet she swore she would remember making love to this man.

His head came up sharply and he swiveled to face her. Piercing blue eyes captured her gaze before they swept down the length of her. She could feel herself blush.

"I couldn't find my clothes," she said as his hot gaze returned to her face. Self-consciously, she brushed her hair out of her face. "Or a brush."

"The clothes, I'd just as soon you do without," the man said with a sexy grin. "But there's a brush on the dresser."

"I think—" she started, her stomach fluttering deliciously at his wicked comment. He stood and advanced toward her but Emily didn't feel fear. Instead, the fluttering increased and she could feel her nipples peak as an ache began between her legs. That did make her take a step back.

"I won't hurt you." His voice was deep and soft as velvet. "You're safe here." He held a hand out and when she didn't move any further, he lightly caressed her bare shoulder. His hand was large and calloused and caused Emily to think all kinds of irrational thoughts. Like hazy memories of those hands on her skin, his lips on hers. This man drew her in with his sexy eyes and voice and she found herself wondering if something had already happened between them.

Still, she hesitated. "How do I know that? I don't know who you are and you don't know me."

"You're Emily and I'm Tyler Sheridan." He stood in the same spot, not advancing but certainly not giving her any space. His eyes slowly slid down her body and back up. She curled her toes under the sagging sheet. "I found you in a snowbank last night. Here in the mountains, possession is nine-tenths of the law, so I guess that makes you mine."

Under normal circumstances, Emily would have been affronted by his audacity, but the smile he gave her when he spoke implied something other than physical ownership. And he knew her name, which meant at some point, she had spoken to him, because she knew she had left her purse in the car.

Howling wind caused her to glance at the windows. She remembered the blizzard. That meant Douglas might not be able to track her. The thought of him sent a shiver up her spine.

"You're cold again. Come closer to the fire." He took her hand and led her over to a huge stone fireplace, the logs crackling brightly and giving off a welcome heat. He sat on the sofa and she turned to sit toward the other end. Unfortunately, her feet got tangled in the sheet and she fell right on top of him.

Tyler wasn't about to let such a great opportunity go to waste. His arms came around her and he lifted his head to kiss her. The minute their lips touched, she surrendered completely, her chest coming to rest on his, her arms circling his neck. He didn't know what it was about her that drew him. From the little she had said, and that was in a cold-induced delirium, she was in trouble. As he came up for breath and began nibbling his way to her ear, he knew he should probably be worried, but the storm would keep any unwanted visitors away from High Ridge for several days.

She gasped as he tugged the sheet down to expose one plump breast. He licked the nipple until it was pebble hard, then gently sucked it into his mouth. Her gasp turned to a moan as she arched her back and exposed more of herself to his questing hands.

"I...I don't want you to get hurt," she whispered as her slender fingers brushed back his hair and she gently kissed his forehead. "I should go."

"The snow..." He peppered her chest with kisses as he made his way to her other breast. "There's no place to go."

"Oh," she said on a sigh just before he reached under the sheet. "Oh!" Her exclamation grew more intense as he cupped her warmth.

"You're hot," he murmured. "So hot." And then he couldn't form a rational thought as he slid a finger through her wetness.

Normally, Tyler could take sex or leave it. Otherwise, he wouldn't be able to live up in the mountains during the winter when more often

145

than not, he and his men couldn't get to town for weeks on end. And after the debacle with his last girlfriend, he hadn't really been looking for a relationship.

He wasn't now, he reminded himself. He just wanted some hot, consuming sex with the incredibly beautiful woman on top of him. And he wanted it now.

In one swift movement, he stood with her in his arms. The sheet fell away but instead of covering herself self-consciously, she reached up with one hand and began undoing the buttons on his shirt. He practically ran to the bedroom.

When he set her down by the bed, she went after his clothes with both hands. No words were needed for them to understand this was a purely physical attraction. When his pants dropped to his ankles and he stood trying to toe off his boots, she sat on the edge of the bed and slid her hands from his neck slowly down his chest, stopping briefly at his nipples and then moving on. His stomach was hard muscle but he sucked it in anyway. He glanced down to see her circle him with one hand and stroke.

Shit, it had been so long, he felt like he was going to explode and he wasn't even inside her. He almost breathed a sigh of relief when she kissed his hip instead, then tilted her head to look at him with a smile. His hands shook as he caught her behind the knees and lifted her legs, sliding into her with one stroke.

She fell back on the bed with a moan, her muscles automatically tightening around him as he began to pump. Not slow and easy, either. Hell no. He rammed into her, meshing their bodies over and over until she cried out in climax.

Surprisingly, her release caused him to slow down. He barely moved within her, wanting to feel the clutch and release of her muscles; wanting to prolong his own orgasm.

"Lock your legs behind me," he said as he leaned over her. When she did, he released her knees and slid both hands up her ribs to her breasts. She had glorious breasts—high and firm and just the right size. She arched her back as he began to knead them, then rocked her hips against his.

"Oh, yeah," he breathed, then sucked one nipple into his mouth as his rhythm matched hers. It wasn't long before he knew he couldn't hold out. She was just too damn hot.

"More," she whispered, then stuck her tongue in his ear. It was all he could take.

With a shout, he climaxed; the hot, gut-wrenching spasms spiraling outward from his groin until he didn't think he could stand. Amazingly, she came again, the deep pull of her muscles sending multi-climactic shudders throughout his entire body.

* * *

Emily had never had simultaneous climaxes in her life. As Tyler crawled up on the bed beside her, she realized what she had been

147

missing. It was awesome, and so thoroughly satisfying she wondered how soon…

"Can we do that again?" she asked, rolling to her side and running a hand across the broad expanse of his chest.

He gave a hoarse chuckle. "If we do, I'll probably die. Hell, I probably just did and don't know it." He turned his head towards her, his eyes glittering in the soft light from the windows. He cupped a hand behind her head and pulled her to him, kissing her lips softly.

"I think we need to talk." He nodded toward the window.

She turned to look, realizing it had stopped snowing.

"Oh, God, I've got to go." She jumped up from the bed, her gaze searching for her clothes. She grabbed her trousers only to find them stiff and scratchy; the result of wool getting wet. "Damn." She tried to tug them on anyway, but the fitted dress pants had impossibly shrunk.

"Here, put these on." Tyler tossed a pair of sweatpants in her direction, and although far too large, at least the elastic kept them up. "Better have one of these, too," he added, handing her a sweatshirt from the drawer he had opened. She jerked it on.

She didn't know what to say. How do you tell a man *thank you very much for the phenomenal sex but I've really got to run?* She ran her fingers through her hair and twisted it in a self-holding knot as she looked for her boots.

"Even though the snow's stopped, it'll be hours, maybe a day or more, before they get the roads cleared." He had shrugged back into his pants and flannel shirt, although the front hung open as he stood there casually watching her frantically try to collect her things. "That is, if you came by car and didn't really drop out of the sky."

"I'm definitely no angel," she huffed.

"Depends on the definition," he replied with that sexy grin of his. "What happened to your car?"

"I slid into a ditch. I really have no idea where."

"Well then, that's settled. Even if they clear the roads, chances are that will just bury your car deeper."

Emily could only hope her car was buried so deeply Douglas wouldn't find it until spring. And maybe when he did, he'd figure she froze to death and would quit looking for her. She glanced around the snug cabin. If she had to hide out from Douglas and his henchmen, at least she had found a great place to do it.

She watched Tyler turn and leave the bedroom, his jeans tight across his butt. Emily supposed she should feel guilty having sex with him when she didn't know him at all, but he had made her feel so wonderful and…safe. If he asked about her circumstances again, she would have to tell him. One fault she had was that she couldn't lie. That's how Douglas had found out what she had done.

"Talk to me," Tyler said later over a second cup of coffee. He had fed her bacon and eggs, but hadn't asked any questions during the meal.

"It would be better if I don't. The less you know—"

"Honey, I need to know what I'm up against."

She looked at those beautiful blue eyes, his chiseled chin, and those hands that had done such wonderful things to her body. Someone had been watching over her last night in the blizzard and had sent Tyler to save her. Did she have the right to drag him deeper into danger by telling him about Douglas?

Tyler reached a hand across the table to cover hers, which he could feel tremble even as she clenched them together.

"Emily, I told you it was safe here. Even when my crew gets the tractor plows out and opens the area around the buildings, nobody can get in without us knowing." He gave her what he hoped was a winning grin. "Besides, what kind of trouble can a beautiful woman like you possibly be in?"

"Have you ever heard of *Omerta*?" she whispered the word.

"What do you know about the code of silence?" He frowned. He knew about the mob's oath of silence that guaranteed death to anyone who spoke against them. His brother had damned near gotten killed because of it while working undercover.

She sighed. "Tyler, you really don't want to know. It would be better if I just left."

"You're not going anywhere, damn it." He didn't raise his voice, but he knew his words scared her. She tried to draw her hands away, but he gripped them tighter, refusing to release her.

"I thought you said I was safe with you," she said, her lower lip trembling. "We had sex, doesn't that mean any—"

"Don't think one had anything to do with the other," he interrupted swiftly. He wiped a hand over his face. How could he make her understand? "I would keep any stranger safe if she landed on my doorstep. But that doesn't mean I would have sex with her. Something entirely different happened when I held you in my arms. Sparks flew and my body ignited like a forest fire. That's all the more reason to keep you safe, not the only one to do so."

The whole time he had been talking, he had kept her hands anchored on the table, but had risen and walked around to where he now stood over her. When she wouldn't meet his gaze, he threaded his hand into her hair and gently tugged, pulling her head back. He looked into eyes filled with tears.

"I don't want you hurt," she whispered, tugging at her hands. This time, he released them and she circled his waist, hugging him close as she buried her face in his stomach. His skin heated instantly as Emily kissed him. He sighed as her lips wandered across his abdomen.

Tyler knew Emily was only trying to distract him, but her lips felt so good that he decided for the moment to let her. He had ways of finding out what the problem was, and if she wouldn't open up to him, he'd just make a call or two. That is, if the lines weren't down from the storm. Figuring that was a good excuse to put off his work, he threaded both hands through her silky hair, enjoying the feel of her lips on his stomach, hoping she would venture lower.

Just as he thought it, her hands drifted down the backs of his thighs, around his knees, and then up the inside of his legs. Her mouth moved just above the waistband of his jeans with hot, moist kisses, but when she got to his belly button, she headed south. He sucked in a breath as she gently bit the bulge in the front of his pants. Nipping down his rigid shaft, she caught just enough skin to make him groan.

As she continued nibbling the tip of him—which for some reason, felt more erotic through his jeans—her hands undid the buttons and then she was sliding his pants down his legs. When he couldn't take anymore, he pulled her up, swiftly taking her place on the chair. He jerked the sweatpants down her legs and she quickly stepped out of them.

"Climb aboard," he invited and was rewarded by a bright smile as Emily straddled his thighs. He gave a sigh and closed his eyes as he felt her heat. When she didn't sheath him, he opened his eyes to find her gaze slowly sliding down his body and back up, her hands traveling the same path.

"You are so gorgeous," she whispered and Tyler could feel his face heat, not used to compliments.

Afraid he would burst if she didn't stop staring at him, he tugged her hips, urging her forward. "Oh, yeah," he rasped as she sank down on him. Keeping his hands on her hips to guide her movements, he slid his thumbs downward, opening her to his touch.

She gasped when he rubbed her and immediately began moving faster. Tyler knew she was close as her inner muscles clutched him, but still he wasn't prepared for her effect on him. Within seconds, he was at the edge. He pressed a little harder and she whimpered, jerking forward as she climaxed, taking him along with her.

It seemed as though he spun in an erotic vortex forever. It wasn't just his male member that felt the clutch and pull of her. His heart hammered, his legs twitched, and his hands trembled. When she collapsed on his chest, it was all he could do to curl his arms around her back, holding her close.

Damn, in less than twenty-four hours, this woman had him bewitched. Even though he knew she could be trouble, nothing mattered except the incredible way she made him feel. Anything else was minor.

Douglas jerked on the extra-large pants and flannel shirt he had stolen out of a trunk in what appeared to be a bunkhouse, shivering when the cold air hit his bare chest. Longing for his cashmere coat instead of the scratchy wool jacket he had to wear, he cursed again.

Damn bitch, this is all her fault.

If only she'd kept her mouth shut and minded her own business. Now, to prove himself to his employers, he had to give up fucking her and kill her.

She had used cash instead of her credit cards to keep him from tracking her, but she wasn't as smart as she thought. He still had a trace on her cell phone through the GPS chip he had installed only last month, and now he had her pinpointed.

He carefully scrutinized the outbuildings of the lumber camp as he trudged to the cookhouse. Well, located to a point. The GPS had led him to a gigantic snow bank where a little digging had uncovered the tail light of her car. He had carefully mounded snow back over it, hoping she was buried inside. He had decided to remain in the mountains a few days just to make sure, and with another blizzard in the making, he had taken refuge at a lumber camp, pretending to be an out-of-luck worker and the foreman had given him a job in the cookhouse.

He snorted, pulling the wool cap low on his head to cover his distinctive blonde hair. Second-in-command of all racketeering east of the Mississippi, and he was working as a fry cook. Yeah, the fucking bitch was going to pay for this.

* * *

"So there you have it," Emily stopped in the middle of the cabin, turning to face Tyler. She had been pacing the living room the entire time she had talked about this Douglas Lattimer character. Though listening carefully to her story, Tyler had been more amused by the way she kept pushing the sleeves of his sweatshirt up her slender arms and hiking up the waist of the pants he had lent her. Personally, he'd just as soon have her prance around naked.

"Well, aren't you going to say anything?" Her question brought him out of his daydream, which had been fast progressing to a wet dream.

"That's it?" he asked. "You have records that could bring down the mob on the entire eastern seaboard, and you're worried?"

"It's not funny," she huffed, wrapping her arms around her midsection. "You can never leave the mob. Unless you're dead," she added in a whisper.

Tyler came to stand in front of her. "Nothing's going to happen. As soon as I can,

155

I'll contact my brother. He's pretty high up in government circles and will know what to do." What Tyler didn't tell her was that his brother, in fact, his entire family, was very well connected. Uncle George was a State Supreme Court Judge and his brother, Harry, was with the FBI. In the meantime, he decided it was time for him to distract her.

"I hear the plows outside, which means the men are clearing a path around the place. Let's find you some warm clothes and take a walk."

"Outside?" Emily squeaked and Tyler could see fear in her eyes. He reached out and cupped her chin, drawing her gaze to his.

"I told you it was safe."

"It's not that. I just…" She sucked in her trembling bottom lip and all Tyler could think of was kissing her until she trembled all over, but in need, not fear.

He gave in to his own need, covering her mouth with his, his tongue sinking deep to savor her sweetness. She immediately softened against him, wrapping her arms around his waist and hugging him tightly. His world tilted wildly as she answered his mating call by sliding her hips against his. Without releasing her mouth, he picked her up and headed for the bedroom. So what if they didn't go for that walk. He could think of plenty of other ways to get exercise.

* * *

It was afternoon by the time Tyler had Emily bundled up enough to venture outside.

"We can stop at the cookhouse and see if Mic has any leftovers," he said as they stepped out into the bright sunshine. "I usually eat with the men and there's always plenty."

"I'm not hungry." Emily let herself feast on the sight of him. She hadn't been able to take her eyes off him when he was naked above her in bed, and even with clothes on, he was a wonder to look at. He wore a bright blue parka, heavy boots, jeans and a pair of wraparound sunglasses. He looked like something out of *Skier* Magazine.

As they trudged down the steps and onto a shoveled path, he tucked her mittened hand into his larger one. He pointed out the various buildings as they walked and she could hear pride in his voice.

"The mill had to be completely rebuilt after a fire about twenty years ago."

"You would have been too young to run this operation then. How did you come to own it?"

"Family. Nobody else wanted to take over from Grandpa. Winters in the mountains were getting too much for him, so he retired to Florida." He shrugged, like owning an operation of this size was an everyday occurrence. He waved in the direction of the other buildings, both with mounds of snow piled as high as the porch and a narrow path coming away from the steps. "Those are the bunk and cookhouse. Are you sure you don't want something to eat?"

As they paused on the path, an unaccountable fission of fear raced down Emily's spine. She nervously glanced around, sure someone was watching her. The cookhouse looked deserted, but a movement at the corner of the window froze her in her tracks. She looked again, the fogged over windows staring eerily back at her.

"Hey, what's the matter?" Tyler stepped into her line of sight, momentarily blocking the brightness of the sun.

She glanced past him but the shadow was gone. A shiver went through her.

"Emily?"

She had to make herself focus on Tyler's voice.

"Are you all right? We can go back if you're cold."

She shook her head, determined not to let him know she was spooked. After all, he had said she was safe here.

"Sorry. I was just thinking that after being stuck in that snowbank, I would have to agree with your grandfather about winters in the mountains."

Tyler wrapped his arms around her and gave her a quick kiss. "Honey, if you spent the winter in the mountains with me, you'd either have the right clothes to keep warm outside or," he paused dramatically and gave her a scorching look, "you wouldn't need anything to wear at all because I wouldn't let you out of my bed."

She held her hands out, palms up. "Hmm. Clothes or no clothes, how's a girl to choose?"

He swatted her playfully on the butt. "Come on. I want to show you the mill."

Together, they walked toward the biggest building on the complex, their boots crunching on the hard packed snow. Emily still couldn't shake the feeling of being watched, so she decided to stick very, very close to Tyler.

* * *

Tyler couldn't get enough of Emily's soft body and giving nature, and for the next two days, they didn't leave his cabin. When he wasn't making love to her in bed, in front of the fireplace, or on the sofa, he took her in the Jacuzzi tub. And it certainly wasn't a one-way street.

Just this morning, he had woken from a very sexy dream to the even more erotic sight of Emily kneeing, her bare butt in the air as she kissed her way down his stomach. He let her have her way with his body for several minutes before he couldn't stand it any longer and let her know he was wide awake. What followed could only be described as every man's wildest fantasy, and the sweet, musky smell of her lingered on his lips as he sat at his desk trying to concentrate on his books.

"Crap." He slammed the ledger shut. Balancing the books at the end of the year was the one part of owning High Ridge he truly hated.

"I can help you with that, you know." Emily walked over. "Why aren't you computerized anyway?"

"Hell, I have trouble doing it the old-fashioned way, much less knowing the computer programs needed."

She leaned her hips against his desk, facing him. "Oh, I don't know. You seem to have a very good grasp on doing it the old-fashioned way." The smile she wore would have a monk stripping, and Tyler was far from monk-like.

He grabbed her onto his lap, sliding the rolling chair back enough so he could prop his feet on the desk. She had no recourse except to fall into him and an instant later, his mouth was on hers and his hand was up the front of her shirt.

"You are insatiable," she gasped when he finally released her from a soul-drugging kiss.

He tweaked her nipple. "You shouldn't offer yourself if you don't want me to take you up on it."

"I offered my services," she replied, then seemed to realize how that sounded and blushed. "I mean my accounting services."

Tyler laughed and slid her off his lap as a knock sounded at the front door. He knew it would be Mic, and the man didn't have the manners to wait before entering.

"Hey, boss. Brought you some lunch." His cook came in, carrying a box covered with a towel. "Ma'am." He nodded at Emily and turned into the kitchen.

Tyler had told Mic about Emily because the cook had accosted him in the mill and asked why he didn't like his cooking anymore. That was definitely not the case, because the men at High Ridge ate very well with Mic in charge of the kitchen. Tyler had arranged with Mic to bring their meals over to the main office, since he didn't want to explain Emily to his men and she seemed to get spooked every time they ventured outside.

"We need supplies," Mic commented when he returned empty-handed. "That blizzard just about leveled my pantry and condiments. All the men wanted to do was eat." Mic actually was a chef from San Francisco but his background and language were in direct variance to his looks. He looked like a biker. He was bald and barrel-chested with multiple tattoos up his arms and across his chest and enough earrings, nose, eyebrow and lip piercings to open his own jewelry boutique.

"Get me a list," Tyler said, knowing he would have to make a trip into town.

"Knew you'd say that." Mic grinned at him, pulling a folded paper from his shirt pocket and dropping it on the desk. "I guess tomorrow will have to be soon enough."

Tyler gave him the eye, but Mic just laughed. He had been with the company since his grandpa ran it, and didn't take shit from anybody. That included Tyler, who liked to think he was boss.

"Do you have to go into town?" Emily asked as he sat her at the table so they could eat.

"You don't want to know what hungry men are like," he replied, scooping mashed potatoes onto his plate and covering them with gravy. He forked some fried chicken from the bowl and passed it to Emily. When she didn't immediately take it from him, he looked up to find her eyes swimming in tears.

"Sweetheart, I'll only be gone a day or two." Knowing she would miss him gave him a warm feeling.

"Maybe I'd better go, too," she said. "See if my car's unearthed and head on down the road."

"No!" At her look, he softened his tone. "I like having you around." He hadn't realized just how much until she spoke of leaving. "Besides, I've called my brother. He's on a case right now but will be here day after tomorrow. I had planned to pick him up in Denver."

She was shaking her head, and he knew he would have to tell her the entire truth.

"Harry's with the FBI. He can help you."

* * *

Later that night, Emily crawled into bed and curled up next to Tyler, who distractedly wrapped an arm around her shoulders as he continued to read a week old newspaper. She knew she was being clingy, but the thought of Tyler not being with her for even a day scared her to death. Mic was the only one at the lumber company she had actually met, but she always felt like she was being watched if they went outside.

"Will Mic bring my meals?" she asked.

Tyler tossed the paper to the floor and rolled to face her. When she wouldn't look at him, he lifted her chin with a finger. "Honey, there's nothing to worry about. Mic will look out for you and I'll be back with Harry before you can miss me." He kissed the tip of her nose.

Emily wanted more. "I miss you already."

"Well, then, let me give you something to remember me by." He took her mouth in a kiss hot enough to melt snow, then spent most of the night giving her a whole lot of memories, the most precious being his soft-spoken "I love you," as he kissed her good-by at dawn.

Emily spent the first day updating Tyler's accounting records, which she had told him she would do. High Ridge was a very profitable business, and the custom-made furniture, though a small part of the lumber mill, was showing steady growth.

When Mic showed up with her supper, she asked if he'd heard from Tyler.

"Nope, and probably won't. Cell phones don't work well up here and the land lines are sporadic in the winter."

That didn't make her feel any better. She told herself Tyler was safe and would be home tomorrow. She just wasn't sure her heart believed it.

That night she was awakened several times when Blackie growled and barked at the door. Tyler had told her to keep the dog inside with her, but now it had her too scared to go investigate. The most she could do was lock the bedroom door and huddle under the covers waiting for morning.

She woke groggy and irritable, feeling only slightly better after her shower.

"If you bark tonight, you're going outside, no matter what." She shook her finger at the dog as she wandered into the kitchen. It wagged its tail and stood expectantly at the door.

Emily let her out and turned to see what Mic had left on the counter for her breakfast. The men started work at dawn so he said he'd leave her breakfast in the kitchen so he wouldn't disturb her. She frowned as she buttered a muffin, wondering why the dog hadn't barked at Mic.

Shortly before ten, she looked up from the ledger when someone knocked at the door. It was too early for lunch. When the knock sounded again, she decided it had to be someone other than Mic and got up to answer it.

She tugged Tyler's flannel shirt closer around her as she walked to the door, breathing in his scent and smiling when she thought of him returning today. She opened the door without thinking.

"Hello, bitch."

With her mind on Tyler, Emily's reflexes were too slow to get the door shut before Douglas barged in. She backed against the wall as he waved a large kitchen knife in her face.

"How did you find me?" She asked the question but knew the answer was irrelevant. Douglas had murder in his eyes. For one brief second, she wished Tyler was there, then just as quickly, was glad he was gone. At least he would be safe.

"Where is it?" he growled, grabbing her by the throat and squeezing. All she could do was shake her head.

"If you give me what I want, I'll kill you fast." He slid the knife down her cheek. "I've been in this godforsaken hellhole for over a week working my ass off while you..." he looked around the cabin, "you've been all cozy and well-fed while you fuck the boss."

Douglas shook her, slamming her head against the wall. Emily saw black at the edge of her vision and willed herself not to faint. The only hope she had was to stay conscious and fight him.

She licked dry lips before she spoke. "I have no desire to return to Chicago, Douglas. Your secret is safe with me if you just leave."

His eyes narrowed and for a minute, Emily thought he might take that deal, but then he laughed. "Yeah, right. I should go merrily on my way when you have business records that can implicate me in numerous crimes." He jerked her forward and pushed her toward the door. "Let's go. I've got plenty of ways to get you to talk once we get back to civilization."

* * *

Tyler walked out of the large garage with his brother just as the snow began in earnest. He turned to enter the cookhouse and tell Mic to have the guys unload his supplies when a movement by his cabin caused his heart to constrict. Emily was being dragged across the yard by a stranger and Tyler could only assume it was Douglas.

"Hey!" he shouted and took off at a run but the snow became so intense, he quickly lost sight of them.

"He's got Emily," he shouted over his shoulder to his brother. "Round up the men!"

He pulled his scarf up over his mouth and nose as he continued to move cautiously forward. He could hear Blackie bark and he moved toward the sound, hoping the dog was following Emily's scent.

Even without much visibility, Tyler had an idea of their direction and his heart pounded. He couldn't let them reach the river. Throwing caution to the wind, he began to run. He had just reached the clearing when the snow stopped and he saw Emily stumble. Adrenalin shot him forward and he tackled Douglas before he could jerk her back to her feet. Blinded by passion and fear for Emily, he swung his fists with all his might. The man stumbled backward and then tumbled out of sight.

"Where'd he go?" Harry had caught up with them and had his handcuffs out.

Tyler jerked off his coat and wrapped it around Emily. When his brother started forward, he grabbed his arm, pulling him backward along with Emily.

"It's too late," Tyler said.

"What?"

He nodded his head toward where Douglas had disappeared. "Listen."

The snow where they had just been standing began to cave in on itself, revealing a rapidly flowing river. Water tumbled over rocks and cut grooves into the snow still packed along the bank.

"His body weight caused the collapse. If the fall didn't kill him on the rocks, the water temperatures will."

He didn't care. All he cared about was the woman who circled his neck when he picked her up and kissed his cheek as he carried her back to the cabin.

* * *

Tyler put Emily to bed and she immediately fell asleep, although she thought he had probably given her a sleeping pill in the water he made her drink. She woke around supper time and followed the voices to the living room.

"It's all taken care of," Tyler's brother said just as she came into the room. Both men stood when they saw her and Tyler put out his hand. She clutched it as they sat on the couch.

"How are you going to protect Emily?" Tyler asked. She knew even with Douglas dead, she wasn't safe.

"We put out the story that their car went out of control and ended up in the river. Lattimer's body was found and will be shipped back to his family." He looked at her with a sheepish expression. "Since Emily has no family, her remains were cremated."

Emily gasped. Tyler put an arm around her shoulders and pulled her close. "Way to go, idiot," he growled at his brother.

Harry shrugged. "Sorry, but it had to be said. Emily?"

She knew what he wanted. She got up and went to get a key from the inside pocket of her coat. "It opens a locker at the bus terminal in Chicago."

"People watch too much TV." Harry shook his head, snorting. "We'll have to get you a new name and identity and relocate you."

Emily nodded. "I always liked my middle name—Nichole," she offered.

"How about Sheridan for a last name?" Tyler spoke softly, giving her a gentle kiss on the forehead.

"But that's your name," Emily protested, and then her heart stopped. Did he mean...

"Yeah," he replied. "Want to share it?"

When Emily had been lost in the blizzard, she had wished to be somewhere warm and wonderful. Now, as she gave Tyler her answer with a kiss, she couldn't think of anywhere more perfectly wonderful than being wrapped in his arms.

The End

If you enjoyed this book, please leave the author a review.

Also by Barbara Baldwin from Books We Love

Hold Onto the Past
Spinning Through Time
A Game of Love
Always Believe
Prospecting for Love
If Wishes Were Magic
Tenderhearted Cowboy
Love in Disguise
An Interlude
Prelude and Promises (coming in November)

Barbara resides in the Midwest but she loves to travel and explore new places, which usually means each of her novels is set in a different locale. She has been published in formats from poetry and short stories to full-length fiction. She really loves writing romance, whether it is contemporary, historical or time travel. She has an MA in Communication and has taught every grade from Kindergarten to college. Visit her website at http://www.authorsden.com/barbarajbaldwin.